The rain not only spoiled the grid and shorted out zapped me with enough juice to hurl me from the top of the bridge. I spied the picnic basket far below me as it hit the river and burst asunder. The way the bits of wreckage floated lazily downstream made the impact seem somehow less traumatic.

Unfortunately, since I was not made of wicker, I was probably going to share the fate of the champagne bottle, which had either sunk straight to the bottom or was smashed to smithereens when it landed.

Another swan dive was out of the question. Even if I'd thought of it in time, my nerves and muscles were still a-jangle from the electric shock and refused to obey me. It probably wouldn't have helped me much anyway. The Fillmore is a pretty high bridge.

I plummeted down, with no way to stop myself, and with the water rushing toward me. I imagined that the impact was going to feel like slamming into a concrete parking lot.

I was wrong.

It felt like slamming into *three* concrete parking lots.

A Mystique Press Production—Mystique Press is an imprint of Crossroad Press.

Copyright © 2021 by Hal Bodner
ISBN 978-1-952979-61-3
For information address Crossroad Press at 141 Brayden Dr., Hertford, NC 27944
www.crossroadpress.com

First edition

FABULOUS IN TIGHTS

HAL BODNER

CHAPTER ONE

Six pairs of eyes looked up at Thanatos with various degrees of fear, anger and desperation. Two more pairs remained closed; provided that he worked quickly enough, they might never reopen.

The lab's ventilation system rapidly filtered out the vestiges of the knock-out gas; the air was soon breathable once again. Thanatos removed his respirator and chuckled when he saw that his victims were now confused as well as terrified. Once they'd regained consciousness, they'd naturally assumed the reason they were trussed up like roasting hens must involve either corporate espionage or flat-out terrorism. While Thanatos' motives certainly encompassed both, he was amused to know that the picture he presented was hardly that of either a spy or a saboteur.

He hummed softly to himself while he ran the electro magnet across the hard drive housings to corrupt the data within. Just to be sure, he subjected the personal laptops of the staff in the same way. He'd already installed a program into the main frame that would target and delete the information he wanted gone. Taken together, the magnet and the software were probably overkill, but it never hurt to be extra careful.

Paranoia was only one of Dr. Bradley Harmon's many irritating personality traits. The scientist habitually refused to share his research with his assistants and technicians until he was absolutely convinced the results were valid. It was only under intense pressure from Jackson Greene, the founder of Greene Genes, that Harmon could be coerced into doling out the information in dribs and drabs, barely enough at any one time to keep his own research teams moving forward.

Harmon's eccentricities would prove to be Thanatos' reward. Once the computers were scrubbed and the lab personnel were dispatched, all records of the Feed the World project, as well as the terrifying potential of the Three-Two-Three genetic variant, would exist nowhere but in Dr. Harmon's head.

And, of course, on the flash drive Thanatos intended to use for his own nefarious purposes.

In spite of the ominous name he had chosen for himself, Thanatos had never killed before. He had always understood, however, that the execution of his plan would almost certainly involve some casualties. Occasionally, he had wondered if a pang of conscience might not strike him at a crucial moment and ruin everything. Now that the time had come, he was mildly surprised that he felt no regret whatsoever for the fates of the eight people huddled helplessly against the wall. The sacrifice of a few PHDs and a handful of technicians was a small price to pay. Even so, to minimize the loss of life, he'd deliberately chosen Centerport's Founders Day celebration as the best time to strike, a time when most Greene Genes employees would be busy setting up for the annual, company-sponsored parade and, thus, out of danger.

Nevertheless, some collateral damage was inevitable. The lab overlooked a huge three-sided courtyard that framed the building's entrance. In the center of the open space, the company had erected a stage where the various floats and bands would pause in order to be judged by the grand marshals. On all sides, covered bleachers had been erected so that the favored spectators could watch the parade in comfort. Several of the peskier members of the Greene Genes Board of Directors should already have taken their seats in the VIP section by now. Those corporate officers and directors whose survival suited his purposes, however, would find their arrivals unaccountably delayed by various means.

The company's CEO, Jackson Greene, would not prove much of an obstacle. The announcement of the old man's impending demise had been distressing, but not unexpected. After decades of exploring arctic tundra, trekking across desolate deserts, and hacking his way through dense jungles in his search for new pharmaceuticals, Jackson's body had finally given out. For decades, the company's founder had ignored the Board's demands for an annual physical, claiming he was far too busy to waste the time fussing with doctors and tests. It was only after he collapsed at a charity function that his doctors discovered the long-dormant tropical diseases that had surged to the fore with such vengeance that there was little modern medical science could do to combat them.

Thanatos had been quick to seize the opportunity.

Copying the data was simple, requiring only a few stolen passwords and some security bypasses. It had been more problematic to smuggle the rest of what he needed out of the Special Projects building, primarily because of the bulk of some of the equipment. The trickiest part by far had been the capture of Dr. Harmon, but Thanatos had not only pulled it off, he'd done it with a certain panache. The scientist was currently squirreled away where there was little chance of anyone coming to his rescue. Once he'd served his purpose, Thanatos would dispatch him as well. Until then, he'd make sure that Harmon was as comfortable as possible under the circumstances.

Once Thanatos completed his final sweep of the room with the magnet, he tossed it aside and spread the rest of the equipment he'd brought with him across one of the lab desks, and got to work. One of the captives had both a clear view of what he was doing, as well as some practical knowledge of what the items were used for. A high-pitched keening came from behind the woman's gag and she thrashed helplessly against the zip ties that bound her wrists and ankles. But escape was impossible, and her panic succeeded only in agitating the other prisoners who remained, for the moment at least, blissfully ignorant of their impending fates.

Thanatos ignored the commotion. Technology, he reflected, was a marvelous thing. It was a belief that, ironically, put him and Jackson Greene in complete accord. Twenty years ago, it would have taken a lot more elbow grease to get the job done. In the modern world, things were much easier.

Thanatos hardly considered himself a demolitions expert.

He felt no shame in admitting that his scientific knowledge was barely more sophisticated than that of a moderately gifted high school student. He did, however, know how to do research on the internet.

It had taken less than an hour to learn how to make something go...*boom!*

CHAPTER TWO

I was having one of those days. Only the need for the Whirlwind to make an appearance could have made things any worse. So naturally...

I was occupied with my least favorite part of my job: Client Relations. It's a euphemism for smoothing the ruffled feathers of the wealthy but touchy old queens that make up the bulk of our business. I had a second call on hold, and I could hear a third line ringing out in the reception area, when my secretary, Randy Whitethorn, flounced into my office in his usual cloud of drama.

"Quick, Alec, hang up! Hang up!"

I winced. If you looked up the word "fey" in the dictionary, you'd find Randy's picture. His most impressive skill was the ability to lisp his way through a sentence which did not contain a single sibilant.

I covered the mouthpiece to mask my exasperation from the client on the other end of the line.

"I'm on with Irving Tressman. You sent him *another* brunette? How many times do I have to tell you...?"

Randy's excitement was instantly replaced by the contrivance of being deeply wounded. He pressed splayed fingers to the center of his chest to make sure I knew how horribly put off he was that anyone would dare question his competence.

"I assure you, dearie, I *never* make the same mistake twice! I sent him the new boy. What's his name? Gary! Blond as a California beach boy with a surf board stomach to match."

"That's wash board, you nit."

"You can surf it if you want," he said archly. "I'll wash. A little soap and all those lovely abs..."

He smacked his lips and fluttered his eyelash extensions. More than once, I'd been tempted to rip them from his eyelids.

"Did you bother to check the drapes to see if they matched the carpet?"

I uncovered the receiver and verbally trampled over Tressman's complaining.

"I know, Irving, I know. I apologize profusely and I swear to you, it will *not* happen again."

I glared at Randy to let him know I was speaking to him as much as to the client. All the while, a torrent of moral outrage poured across the telephone wires. Irving Tressman is one of those people who believe that volume is the secret to getting what they want. When he called on his cell, he was sometimes so loud that the tower couldn't keep his voice from distorting. Unfortunately, he was calling from a land line at the moment, and I was clearly able to discern the phrases "dissatisfied customer," "entitled to compensation," and "over-rated reputation," all hurled across the wires at several thousand decibels.

My temper bristled at that last bit. Given the nature of my business, I can be prickly when someone calls my reputation into question. Even though Mayor Richie Banterly had legalized prostitution, there were still people who looked down their noses at the Archer Agency. Fortunately, Marilyn Cramer over at Boy Toys took most of the heat from the religious types, probably because she ran women as well as boys. A lot of people find the idea of male hookers to be glamorous. You'd be surprised how many bored housewives and frustrated career women are titillated by the prospect of a hot stud paid to indulge their every sexual whim, while many unattractive men thrill to the fantasy that only a few extra pounds and a gym membership stand in the way of their career as a professional gigolo.

Where male prostitutes are concerned, both sexes have delusions of glamor.

But when it comes to female sex workers, people get touchy, partly because the media loves to highlight sex slavery and kiddie porn. The last time I had lunch with Marilyn, she wanted my advice on how to make sure her clients understood that her girls were in the business voluntarily, and that they were handsomely paid. Short of posting copies of her employees' 1099s, I couldn't come up with anything.

But that's not the reason the Archer Agency's employees are all male. It has nothing to do with the moral backlash. On the contrary, on the Kinsey Scale, which only goes up to six, I'm an eight. Even the thought of accidentally seeing a pair of bare titties makes me break out into a cold sweat.

Speaking of sweating, Tressman's bitching was making me more than a little hot under the collar. Though a dozen archly vitriolic comebacks were on the tip of my tongue, I wrestled my temper into control. Notwithstanding his many personality flaws, and his lack of interpersonal skills, Irving Tressman was still one of my best clients. I took a deep, steadying breath and forced myself to be politic.

"I'll tell you what I'm going to do for you, Irving..."

I continued to glare at Randy while I spoke. Obviously, I couldn't voice any of the more creative threats I had in mind, not while Tressman was able to overhear; they might turn him on. On the other hand, I was doing my best to silently communicate that, as soon as I hung up on the old poof, adding bleach to Randy's high-colonic rinse was not entirely out of the question.

"I know it can't begin to make up for the mistake..."

Even to myself, I sounded as unctuous as a television evangelist. But Irving wouldn't give a damn about my insincerity as soon as he understood that he might get something for nothing.

"...perhaps you'll accept a gift? To apologize for any inconvenience we caused you."

I imagined Irving's ears tilting forward like a mangy, obese hound who had caught the scent of a rabbit– preferably already stewed so that he wouldn't have to exert himself by running it down. Sure enough, Tressman quieted enough to listen.

"I see you have Matthew booked for tomorrow night. How would you feel about us sending you *both* Matthew and...?"

I paused to heighten Tressman's anticipation. Though I'd never admit it to Randy's face, there are a few useful techniques I've picked up from my secretary's dramatics.

"...David."

There was an involuntary gasp from the other end of the phone which Tressman was not *quite* able to suppress. I added, as if the question wasn't rhetorical, "You *do* remember him, I hope?"

When Tressman began to gush about exactly *how* he remembered David, including some intimate details I could have happily ended my days without ever hearing, I knew we were out of the weeds without too much damage. I refrained from retching, and made appreciative noises, while Irving boasted of his sexual prowess. In the meantime, Randy tried to get my attention by waving his arms like an over-sexed peacock parading its feathers for a whole harem of hens.

"You don't say?" I crooned. "*Three* times! At *your* age? Irving, you old stud! I *never* would have guessed it."

Admittedly, Randy croons better than I do but I'm working on it.

"I want to make absolutely certain that David will…ahem… *fill* your needs. I know he's shorter than you normally like. Since we don't want to make another mistake, if you'd rather have someone taller…?"

Tressman hastened to assure me that there was no need to dwell on past mistakes, and that he'd be just fine spending the evening with the pair.

Matthew wouldn't be a problem. The kid would hump an ostrich in Macy's window if it paid well enough. David, though, was another matter. He'd been less than thrilled with Tressman on their first date, and it was going to be a chore to get him to accept the assignment. Apparently, though it boggled the mind to imagine it, Irving Tressman was even more difficult when he was naked than he was when he was fully clothed. Rather than admit to his own impotence, the balding jeweler liked to take his frustrations out on the hired help. Even though my employees, of necessity, are trained to handle that kind of thing, I don't expect them to tolerate abuse from an old queen who expects someone else to take the blame for his inability to get it up.

Luckily, one of my guys had discovered that Tressman had a foot fetish. Sucking the old poof's toes was good for half an erection at least. I'd dutifully written the information down. If any of the boys fails to review the notes in a client's file before a date, they have no one to blame but themselves.

With Randy's gesticulations growing grander by the minute, I assured the jeweler that, come Friday night, I could guarantee a two-for-one special that would blow, if not his mind, than at least something. With that, I rang off and turned my attention to Little Miss Drama Queen.

"I had *no* idea it was a dye job!" he protested in high dudgeon. "I *must* find out who he uses. It was *that* good."

"You didn't check."

Randy's swarthy, attractive features were twisted into a mask of outrage worse than if I'd accused him of having hadBotox treatments. Though he claimed that his mother was one half Cherokee, and though his skin was certainly bronzed enough to suggest Native American blood, I had always suspected that he was actually Puerto Rican.

"You *honestly* don't expect me to get *close* enough to go over them with a *magnifying glass*, do you?"

I wouldn't have been surprised if he'd confessed to doing just that as part of the standard interview process.

"I expect you to make sure that a blond is a blond is a blond. Especially when the guy is booked by Irving Tressman. You make them strip during the interview, right? At least to the waist?"

"I have them do more than that," Randy's eyes glazed at some choice memory. "In this business, size matters after all."

"After taking all that care," I asked sarcastically, "how did you manage to miss this?"

He fixed me with another arch look, tilting his head back and gazing at me down the length of his pseudo-aristocratic little nose. "As I *just* said...size matters. I was *distracted* by my *examination* of other things."

He plucked a tissue from the holder on my desk and dabbed delicately at the corner of his mouth. The gesture was calculated to get under my skin. Though I sometimes found Randy's incessant verbal innuendos amusing, he knew I drew the line at outright crudeness.

Even all those years ago when Richie Banterly and I were

working the same street corners, I always tried to keep things classy. The two of us had reputations for being clean, and not just because we bathed regularly. We obeyed informal rules, which we set for ourselves, which dictated that we avoid drugs, and never drank anything stronger than a single cocktail or a beer or two while we were working. When you're hooking on the street, you never know when you might need to rely on a friend if a trick turns sour. You want to make sure your lifeline isn't someone who's tweaked to the tits or falling down drunk. Richie and I had a pact to watch each other's backs.

Most people snickered when Richie decided to run for mayor. To his advantage, he was young, passionate, intelligent, and committed. He brought a fresh vibrancy to Centerport's political scene and, I guess, the citizens figured that if they were going to have a whore in the Mayor's office, it might as well be someone who was up front about it. The incumbent, whose tenure as mayor had been riddled with corruption, was as surprised as anyone else when Richie won by a wide margin.

One of Richie's first orders of business had been to "clean up" the red-light district, not because he had a moral problem with it, but because he was tired of seeing young people like us being exploited. He had cracked down on the drugs, the pimps, and the violence. He'd gotten the under-aged kids off the streets and into facilities that could help make sure they stayed off. But he knew he couldn't eliminate the trade entirely, so he'd done the next best thing.

He legalized it.

Then, he taxed it and regulated it. And, finally, he'd reached out to a few people he trusted to help legitimize it. If hookers were a fact of life, Richie wanted to make sure that the hookers in *his* town would be well paid, protected, healthy and, above all, safe. Richie figured that escort agencies, set up as legitimate businesses, were the way to go.

I was one of the first people he'd approached to help him out. To be honest, I was hesitant at first. What did I know about running a business? At the time, I had enough regular clients to keep me in "cigarettes and nylons" as the drag queen friend of mine used to say. I also had a somewhat unusual inheritance from my late parents, so I didn't have to worry about making rent. In short, I was perfectly content to have worked my way up from a street hooker into a fairly high-priced call boy.

I had also just met Peter.

Pete knew what I did for a living. In fact, that was how we met. He'd been steadily climbing the corporate ladder at Greene Genes and when he finally nailed a position on the Board, a few of his friends decided to rent him a professional to celebrate. That professional was me. And I can happily state that the nailing went on for a great many more hours than his friends had paid for. It never bodes well for a prostitute to fall for a client; at the Archer Agency I have strict rules against it. With Peter though, it was a magic, once in a lifetime, love at first sight kind of thing. We've been together ever since.

Even so, Peter and I were both aware that it wasn't a great idea for a rising corporate *wunderkind* to be married to a hooker. If I were a *businessman*, however, I could pass as respectable. At least on the surface. Fortunately, between the cash and properties I'd inherited, launching the Archer Agency was a do-able next step. Peter wasn't thrilled that I'd embarked on a new career as a male Madam, but he reluctantly accepted it. To my surprise, I discovered I had a pretty good head for business. In a remarkably short period of time, the Archer Agency was a big success.

That's not to say that my profession wasn't sometimes a burden on our relationship. Peter steadfastly refused to come out at work. Though some of his colleagues must have known he was gay and simply chose not to make a big deal out of it, the fact that he was married to the owner of a brothel wouldn't be quite as easy to ignore. The need for secrecy rankled with me, but it's amazing the things you can put up with when you truly care about someone.

"If you've *completely* finished *berating* me..."

Randy's comment snapped me out of my reverie and erased the sappy look from my face, the one that I got whenever I was thinking about my husband.

"...I came in to tell you..."

He sashayed to the window behind my desk and opened

the blinds. I couldn't help reflecting that with his tight, gymnast build and that darkly brooding, handsome face, I could have made a fortune from him if only he wasn't so damned nelly. With a sigh for lost business opportunities, I swiveled in my chair, looked out the window, and saw chaos reigning only a few blocks away.

Columns of oily black smoke partly obscured the view, pierced by a huge gout of flame that soared toward the sky and gave off spirals of sparks. Now that Tressman was no longer yelling in my ear, I could dimly hear sirens in the distance. A sharp shard of tension speared me in the pit of my stomach, even though I realized it was only my imagination that made it sound like people were screaming as well.

"It's the Green Genes Special Projects Building. It's all over the news," he told me with ghoulish excitement. Then, legitimate concern flashed across his face and he asked, "Peter doesn't...?"

"No," I said.

Peter's office was in the main corporate building several blocks further down on Overmeir Street. Besides, he'd planned to spend the afternoon at the hospital with his boss, Jackson Greene. Jackson and Peter had a strong relationship that transcended business; Jackson was his mentor as well as his boss. After the old man got the latest test results back, Peter wanted to be at his side to help him cope with the bad news.

"There are hundreds of worker bees still inside," Randy continued. "Even worse..."

He lowered his voice to a somber whisper and shuddered to highlight the awfulness of the tragedy.

"...The parade!"

He gave me a knowing look, as if I should know what he was taking about.

"What parade?"

He feigned shock at my ignorance, even though he'd probably been expecting it, and barreled on, relishing every detail as only a man who has inherited the gossip chromosome from both parents can.

"My dear! Do you *never* pay attention to anything that happens in this town?"

If Randy only knew how much attention I was forced to pay...

"Today is the Founders Day parade. The biggest private sponsor is..." He paused for unnecessary dramatic impact, "... Green Genes!"

He closed his eyes and inhaled deeply through both nostrils, as if bracing himself against the horrors he felt compelled to describe with gruesome gusto.

"The parade route goes right through the courtyard of the Special Projects Building so the judges can get a good look at all the floats. There was an explosion and... Well, it's all too, too horrible to think about!"

He fanned himself with a piece of paper he took from my desk. Sadly, there was no fainting couch on hand, or he'd have probably used it.

"The news says there are people still trapped in the building. Flaming furniture keeps falling down onto the crowd and..."

He opened his eyes to display pupils dilated with excitement. His cheeks had colored, and he kept punctuating each sentence with gasps of affected horror. It had the unpleasant effect of letting me know what he probably looked like when he was on the verge of an orgasm.

"Terrible, my dear. Just terrible."

"You are one morbid queen, do you know that?"

Randy isn't truly malicious, he's simply the quintessential Drama Queen. While he can be as catty as hell, he's also been known to burst into tears when he sees a TV commercial soliciting donations for starving orphans. The weeping builds to a crescendo, but after he's wrung the last bit of sympathy for himself out of whoever's watching television with him, he never fails to send a check to UNICEF. He'll also keen like an Irishman at the tragic plight cinema heroines, especially when said heroine is played by Bette Davis, Olivia De Havilland, or one of the other mid-century divas he emulates. Of course, to disguise the fact that he actually has a heart, he's spent years honing his tongue until it's sharp enough to slash tires at fifty paces,

Words failing him—an occasion to celebrate in itself—he

huffed to show he was above my insults, and he switched on the wall-mounted TV. Images of costumed revelers fleeing the area filled the screen. An announcer's voice babbled incoherent details with thinly disguised panic. The camera panned upward to show flame spouting from broken windows eight stories above the street. Even as we watched, part of the brick facade of the building bulged outward and collapsed, raining more death onto the people below.

"Turn that off," I snapped.

I had to get Randy out of my office. Quickly.

"How can you *not* be interested, Alec? It's your *husband's* company!"

"My husband is safe and sound. Short of throwing on a yellow slicker and joining the fire brigade, there's nothing I can do, is there?"

My callousness was complete pretense but, hopefully, Randy would latch onto the opportunity to be even more offended and flounce out of the office so I could do what I had to do.

"On the other hand, since it's *your* fault that I had to double-book David for tomorrow night, if you don't get to work straightening out the schedule, I swear I will put mentholated rub into that jar of personal lubricant you keep in the bottom drawer of your desk."

"How did you...?" He acted appalled, as if I'd discovered his deepest secret.

"The Shadow knows," I said. I fixed him with a steely glare and added in a tone that brooked no argument, "Next time, check the roots. *All* of them."

Grumbling under his breath about how little I appreciated him, Randy traipsed out. As soon as he'd slammed the door, I reached under my desk and flipped the switch that was hidden there. My office door locked with a click. Simultaneously, the glass in the wall of windows behind my desk polarized. As soon as I was sure no one could see in, I shifted the desk blotter and pressed my palm to the scanner hidden underneath. A soft beep sounded and the wet bar on the far wall slid soundlessly behind the bookshelves to reveal a small elevator. Though a humble blotter might seem like a flimsy cover, I had no fear that my secret would be discovered. Randy was the only person allowed in my office when I wasn't there, and he would rather sleep with a woman than lift a finger to clean anything. The thin layer of dust coating both the blotter and the desk were as much of a protection as they were an irritation.

The car descended swiftly into a basement which failed to appear on any of the building's blueprints. Travis Buttrick might resemble a cross between a grizzly bear and a homeless person, but in spite of how intimidating he looks, he has a network of people eager to do him favors including, it seemed, cronies in Centerport's Urban Planning department. He's also one of the smartest people I've ever met when it comes to electronics and computers. He's constantly creating new gadgets and concocting mysterious chemical substances to help me out. Unfortunately for me, he usually fails to take into account that there's an actual person who has to operate his contraptions and wear his gadgets and, as a result, he doesn't always design them with my comfort in mind. In fact, sometimes I think he makes things deliberately awkward for me, just to keep me on my toes.

Purely by happenstance, I discovered that even Travis' genius can't overcome a quart of Tom Kha Kai soup accidentally spilled on one of his inventions. In my defense, I *never* claimed to be graceful. Now though, whenever he summons me to help him "test out something new," if at all possible, I stop by a Thai restaurant first and bring take-out into the lab.

Changing into the costume rarely takes more than a minute as getting dressed and undressed quickly is one of the skills I retained from my years as a fancy boy. Travis made the original outfit out of wool. The instant I began to perspire, it felt like my entire body had jock itch. Though I heal almost instantly from most things, it was horribly uncomfortable the entire time I wore the thing.

I complained. Travis told me I was being a baby and ignored me. I complained some more. Ditto. It was only after a reporter snapped a shot of me with my hands down the front of my tights, scratching the devil out of my crotch, that Travis relented. He brags that my current suit is some kind of scientific marvel. As far as I'm concerned, it's virtually indistinguishable from Spandex.

The first time I put it on, I thought it lacked only a tutu and an orchestra playing *Swan Lake* to keep it from being completely ridiculous. But once I got used to it, I couldn't help admiring the way it clung to me like a second skin and made my muscles look even better than they did when I stood, bare-chested, in front of the mirrors in the gym locker room. Unfortunately, I'd never be able to model it for Peter.

Travis assured me that the material is fireproof, tear proof, bullet proof, and could withstand a terrific amount of pressure which, I suppose, will come in handy if I'm ever in danger of being squeezed to death by a giant squid. From experience, I knew three of the other claims were true. As for the last one, Travis keeps nagging me to let him fire a gun, point blank, into my chest. He pretends to misunderstand when I make excuses.

All in all, the suit is really pretty nifty. It has only one minor drawback.

It triggered a minor fetish that I'd never known I had.

There's something about the way the material clings to my skin, silky and smooth, sleek and shiny. It's like being oiled up for the beach or competing in a wet T-shirt contest without having to go through the inconvenience of getting wet or oily. To be frank, wearing it is a turn on. And yet, I know it's not cool for Centerport's resident superhero to go around rescuing damsels in distress–or young knights in peril, for that matter– with a raging hard on. Luckily, most of the time I wear it, I'm much too busy staying alive to be aroused. It's only when I'm *en route* to a crisis that I have to worry about the outline of my dick showing.

I quickly ducked my head under a machine that darkens my hair from reddish-gold to a dark chestnut. I keep telling Travis we could market it and corner the market on women's hair coloring, but he refuses to listen. In the beginning, we experimented with a cowl, but it was more trouble than it was worth. My vision and hearing are completely normal; with the hood covering my ears, everything was muffled. Any chance of tricking a supervillain into revealing the details of his nefarious plans would be severely hampered if I had to keep asking him to repeat himself. As a finishing touch, I don a mask and my transformation into the Whirlwind is complete.

In spite of the many arguments we have, one thing Travis and I are in complete agreement about is the need to protect Peter.

No one knows what it is about Centerport that's so attractive to arch villains but for decades it's been a magnet for them to launch their evil schemes. Every year, the city sees its share of costumed crazies bent on world domination, or revenge, or garden variety psychosis. Some of them are in it for the money, some lust for power, and others have distinct goals that, while hard to fathom at first by normal standards, make perfect sense once you look at things from the bad guy's warped point of view.

Some of them are simply bat-shit crazy. And vicious. And seeking revenge against anyone who has thwarted them in the past; anyone like the Whirlwind. They'd get a kick out of using Peter to get to me. Knowing what some of those loons are capable of, my mind balks at what could happen if they discovered the connection between us. Travis and I take every precaution to make sure that no one *ever* sees me exiting the Archer Agency's building in my superhero drag. We're even more careful about not letting any of the bad guys find out about Peter, so even in the direst emergencies, the Whirlwind rarely comes and goes from Ale Mary's, the old nightclub where Peter and I live.

There's an abandoned subway tunnel that runs underneath both my office building and the club. Roughly midway between the two lies a warehouse that Travis picked up cheap. It used to house the Drinky-Winks Soda Pop Company. Before that, it was the Dirty Doings Diaper Depot, a laundry that catered to new mothers in the days before disposables were invented. I've always suspected that the lingering odor might be the reason the soft drink company folded. The only thing worse than drinking overly sweet carbonated water might be drinking overly sweet carbonated water that tastes faintly of baby shit.

I darted through the tunnel and emerged from a concealed door in the side of the Drinky-Winks building that opens onto an alley. Even through the press of the tall buildings looming on both sides, I saw oily black smoke darkening the sky.

At a trot that was faster than most professional track athletes could run full-out, I was halfway across town in mere minutes. As I got closer to the disaster zone, I had to slow down in order to shoulder my way through the crowd of lookie-loos who were gathered behind the police barriers and pointing up at the building with unsuppressed excitement. The Whirlwind's costume is bright turquoise with yellow piping; it's pretty hard to miss. Yet even though most of the onlookers knew exactly who I was and, presumably, why I was there, they still refused to get out of the way. A few even had the gall to ask me for an autograph which just goes to prove that some people have absolutely no sense of occasion.

I finally pushed my way up to the police barrier. The days when I needed to alert Police Chief Gretchen Thatcher that I was on the scene were long behind me. One of her officers would have already spotted the flash of turquoise and let her know I was around.

I looked up at the conflagration, which was still going strong. Though the Special Projects building was certainly no skyscraper, it was still pretty high. I had no idea how I was going to put out a fire of this size and save any people who were trapped inside–especially if they were on the higher floors. But I didn't let that bother me much. Once I got inside, I knew something would occur to me.

Something always does.

Well, *almost* always.

CHAPTER THREE

"My god! All those people! Those poor, poor people!" Jackson had one hand clapped over his mouth in horror; his eyes remained riveted to the television screen.

"Does anyone have any idea how it happened?"

"First guess is that it was an explosion in the main labs on the fifth floor. We're not absolutely sure yet."

With his back to the duty nurse, Peter Camry surreptitiously filled the plastic water tumbler with scotch from a pint-sized silver flask, and handed the drink to his boss. The doctors had advised the old man against drinking alcohol, but given the prognosis, Jackson ignored them. The single-malt could hardly do much more damage to his ravaged system and, since he was dying anyway, Jackson didn't particularly care if it did. He'd spent a lifetime trying to unlock Nature's secrets, using Her bounty to create new pharmaceuticals and to advance biomedical science, all at the expense of paying attention to his own health. Looking back across a career that had provided so many benefits to humanity, he didn't regret a single fever or ague, not one parasite or infection. If that was the price he had to pay for the betterment of Mankind, so be it.

His only regret was that there was still so much more to do, so many new discoveries to make. So many projects that he would never see to completion.

"I got the company helicopter into the air as soon as I heard." Peter interrupted the old man's reverie. "They've been taking people off the roof. But they don't know how long they can keep it up. The heat's getting worse and they tell me there are...updrafts?"

Jackson nodded and clutched his glass of scotch in a white-knuckled hand. "I know what they are. Go on."

"It's getting harder to land but the pilots are doing their best. On the ground though..." Peter shook his head sadly.

"The Founder's Day parade!" Jackson's eyes widened.

Since they'd started watching the news, the cameras had been focusing more on the burning building than on the crowds below.

"Chief Thatcher cleared the area as soon as she could. Most of the spectators fled but..."

His voice trailed off and Jackson thought he saw a sorrow that mirrored his own in the younger man's eyes.

"But...what?"

"A chunk of the building's facade came down before anyone knew what was happening. I'm afraid...well...it crushed the grandstand, Jackson. I'm sorry."

Greene felt his mouth grow dry and had to swish some of the scotch around to moisten his tongue before he could continue. "We sponsored that parade. Our people..." He swallowed again, dry, this time. "Who...? Who did we lose?"

Peter was reluctant to speak.

"Please, Peter. I must know."

Peter sighed and dropped into a chair. Once again, his eyes roved over the frantic messages scrolling across his phone's screen but he already knew what they said. There was no point in delaying any further.

"Mallory Foster and Jacob Eisenberg are confirmed dead."

"My god! My god!" Jackson kept repeating throughout the recitation.

"Ambrose Cole is missing. We should assume the worst. Fortunately, Gary Montague was held up in traffic and didn't get there until after the explosion. He's been texting me from the site as he gets new information. Prudence was badly burned. She's been taken to hospital but..." He shrugged, sadly. "She may not survive."

"And Herman?"

Peter couldn't suppress a snort. It was no secret that Herman Starcke, the Greene Genes CFO, despised him.

"Sorry." He blushed apologetically at Jackson's stern glance. "Herman was against sponsoring the parade from the beginning. Lucky for him, he was boycotting it. Lucky for us, they wanted to keep you here a few extra days. Otherwise..."

"You and I would have been there too." Jackson shook his head. "I *should* have been there," he spat bitterly. "Seventy-nine years old with only a few months left. It should have been me instead of the others. They had so much more to contribute to the world whereas I..."

"Stop it, Jackson." Peter's harsh tone cut through the other man's misery.

Peter had no doubt that Jackson would have willingly thrown himself into the pyre if it meant the others could have been saved; the old man was truly that altruistic. Given the current crisis, neither of them could afford to succumb to emotion. Herman Starcke certainly wouldn't. Everything Jackson had worked for—everything Peter had worked for—was in too much jeopardy. At the moment, grief would be an indulgence.

He rose to place a reassuring hand on the old man's shoulder.

"Your death would have only made things worse. The cost in human loss is, of course, terribly steep. But the loss of *your* vision..." He gently squeezed and felt the wasted muscle beneath his fingers. "Greene Genes *still* needs you for whatever time you have left. Especially now."

"Nonsense. You're quite capable of rebuilding without me, Peter. Almost half the board—gone! Old friends, all of them," he moaned.

"I wasn't talking about that." There was worse news to come and Peter felt an obligation to break it to him as gently as possible. Jackson waited while Peter resumed his seat.

"I had hoped...*we* had hoped..." the young man continued.

He wasn't exactly sure what effect the news would have and he proceeded cautiously, just in case. He needed to tell his boss what had happened, but he wanted to phrase it in such a way that Jackson would agree to the solution Peter had devised.

"Yes?"

"I know how much you'd hoped to witness the success of the Feed the World Project. We were so close."

Understanding dawned. "The labs," Jackson whispered with deep angst.

Peter Camry nodded. "Brad Harmon is gone. He got back into town last night. The explosion happened first thing this morning."

"Is there any chance...?"

"How long have you known Brad? Can you imagine him being so much as five minutes late on his first day back at work? We had to practically browbeat him to take the damned vacation in the first place." Peter chuckled, but there was no mirth in it. "No, I'm afraid he perished along with everything else."

"What about his research? I had him to dinner the night before he left for Tahiti. He spent half the meal trying to get me to let him cancel the trip, and the rest of it babbling about some major breakthrough he'd made."

"Did he give you any details?"

Jackson waved his hand to dismiss the notion. "Bradley? Hardly. He never said anything until he was damned good and ready. Just hints and teases. You know how he was. All I got from it was that, with luck, within a decade we might be able to end world hunger once and for all." A thought occurred to him. "Surely we have back-ups of everything?"

"Yes." Peter was reluctant to meet Jackson's gaze. "And no."

"What do you mean?" Jackson Greene's aura of command, though weakened by illness, was still formidable, "Dammit, Peter. Look at me."

Camry fidgeted. To Jackson's eye, it looked incongruous on someone who was usually so self-composed. Peter's fingers fluttered against his phone screen while his boss waited impatiently for an answer.

"We have most of the background information. It's standard operating procedure to store copies of everything that Special Projects does off-site."

"On the mainframe in the basement of the corporate building. Yes, yes. I know that."

"Bradley, though, well, he was never one to pay much attention to procedure." Peter spread his hands helplessly. "We've only just started checking but, so far, it doesn't look like he made any recent entries into the system. My guess is that he kept all the new data on his personal laptop."

"He always was a stubborn cuss," Jackson muttered with affection.

"He wasn't working in a vacuum, so he must have shared some of it with his staff. But he never let the right hand know what the left one was doing. Not that it matters now." Peter shook his head. "He scheduled a staff meeting for this morning. I guess he wanted reports on what's been happening while he was away. They were all there. *With* their computers. I'm sorry Jackson. Whatever inspiration he had, it's gone now."

"The loss," the old man moaned. "Not just to those poor people who died in this...this...horrible accident but, to the *world*! What are we going to do?"

He struggled not to sob. Peter sat by, looking at him with sympathy until Jackson had control of his emotions once again. The younger man cleared his throat softly a few times before proceeding. He'd been planning this moment for months, waiting for the right opportunity to bring up the subject. Given Jackson's condition, it was now or never.

"Actually, I've been wondering how to talk to you about this for a while and, well, this disaster forces my hand."

He paused as if uncertain, or even afraid, to continue. Again, Greene found this unusual behavior for his protegee; he'd never known Peter to hesitate about anything. In fact, the young man's ability to think quickly and make decisions in a crisis, decisions which, more often than not, ended up being the correct ones, were some of the qualities Jackson most admired in him.

"You may think this terribly callous of me." Camry motioned toward the tragedy playing out on the television screen. "I'm just as upset as anyone else about what's just happened. But I can't afford to give in to grief. *We* can't afford it. I'm not talking about money. The greater good of humanity is at stake."

"Go on."

Peter dropped to one knee, and took one of Jackson's hands into his own. Backslapping and youthful locker room horseplay notwithstanding, Jackson had never been comfortable with physical intimacy between men. That he was aware of Peter's sexual persuasion, though the two of them had never discussed it openly, made it even harder to avoid flinching. Nevertheless, he was reasonably sure he'd never revealed how awkward it made him feel to his protegee.

"Let me take over the project."

"What?" Whatever Jackson had expected, this was certainly not it. "Why in heaven's name would you want to do that? Without Bradley, it's doomed."

"Stop being so negative," Peter chided with a hint of a rueful grin. "I know you want me to take the helm when...well... when..."

"When I die. You needn't mince words. I'm not happy about it but there's nothing I can do. I've never made a secret about who I want to take my place. I can go to my grave happy, knowing you'll be faithful to my vision."

"That's just it."

Jackson wasn't sure he approved of how quickly Peter wanted to discuss business, not with the carnage still taking place only blocks away. Nevertheless, he understood passion, especially the passion for discovery; it had driven him for most of his life.

"As of today," Peter continued, "there are vacant seats on the board. You know as well as I do that Herman's already girding his loins and preparing for battle. He'll want to fill them with his people. Herman Starcke doesn't care about benefitting mankind. He's motivated strictly by profits."

Jackson Greene, for all his visionary attributes and, some might say, his naivete about making the world a better place, was far from a stupid man. Though he'd never before been faced with a setback quite as devastating as the cataclysm they were witnessing, he was no stranger to disaster. He forced his grief into abeyance long enough to assess the situation as objectively as he could.

"With Mallory, Ambrose, and Jacob gone..." he mused.

"And very probably Prudence."

"Herman still has a power base but..."

"...It's not as strong," Peter finished for him. "Those board vacancies are key. If I could somehow manage to pull Feed the World out of the fire..."

Peter's face flushed and he started to stammer as soon as he realized he'd been tactless given what they were watching. Jackson smiled grimly to let him know he understood there was no ill intent behind the words.

"I mean...I already have some ideas on how to salvage this. If I can do it..."

"Success goes a long way with any board. Inheriting my stock interest won't hurt either."

"I can carry out your vision, Jackson." Peter's eyes lit with a zealot's glow. "You may not be here to see it, but you can imagine it. No one need go hungry ever again! After that, there's the Ocean Reclamation program. Research to fight antibiotic-resistant bacteria. All those clean fuel projects that have been languishing. If I can make Feed the World work, no one will pay any attention to Herman's nay-saying. We could *finally* do the things we've always dreamed of."

"Make absolutely sure you want to do this, my boy." There was doubt in Greene's voice. "If you fail..."

"I will *not* fail you, sir. I swear!"

Jackson Greene remained lost in thought for several moments. In the end, he couldn't deny Peter the opportunity to prove himself. Besides, to the young man's credit, he had never failed to come through before, often to Jackson's surprise.

"Very well. But first..." He held up a single finger to stress the point he was about to make. "You get down to that accident site and see what you can do to help." He saw Peter's reluctance to leave him and added, "I'll be *fine*. Reviving Feed the World is going to take a minor miracle. Start showing me what miracles you can work by doing your best to help as many of those poor souls as possible. Now go."

Peter Camry was out the door in a flash. Jackson Greene took a deep breathe, trying to hold himself together. But within seconds of his gaze returning to the television screen, the old man began to sob.

CHAPTER FOUR

The courtyard of the Special Projects Building was engulfed in chaos. Fortunately, Gretchen's cops had confined the onlookers behind barriers placed well back from the chunks of flaming wreckage that were still tumbling down from five floors above. Very little remained of the grandstand but a heap of splintered wood, crushed metal and torn bunting. Even as I watched, the rescuers were forced to pause their search for the injured and the dead because a huge chunk of concrete fell from above to obliterate what was left of the bleachers. The street leading to the courtyard had been turned into an impromptu triage area and the EMTs had their hands full.

In spite of how well organized the first responders were, there were still panicked people running around like chickens with their heads cut off, either too terrified or too stupid to worry about dodging debris. A sporadic exodus of shell-shocked Greene Genes employees trickled out of the building's main entrance, many of them assisting more severely burned and injured coworkers to safety, while others raced pell mell into the courtyard, their heads covered with their hand, their laptops, coats, or sheaves of paper, as if any of them would provide protection from the crumbling debris above them. A few people were huddled on the curb in fetal positions, while others wandered aimlessly, ignoring barked orders from the police to stand clear of the building. One woman stood ramrod straight with her fists clenched at her sides, screaming at the top of her lungs. All the veins in her neck stood out from the strain of maintaining the volume.

The worst part of trying to rescue civilians is usually the

civilians themselves. There's no kind or polite way of telling them to shut up, hang limp, and let themselves be rescued. Too many of them insist on trying to help you help them and end up making things worse. My biggest pet peeve is that there's always one, one person who demands to be the center of attention, even though they're virtually uninjured. You know the type. The self-absorbed businessman who complains about the damage to his new BMW while the paramedics are trying to save the lives of the people in the battered Toyota he hit because he felt he was too important to yield. The spoiled kid who blubbers dramatic crocodile tears at the scene of someone else's tragedy to improve her chances of going viral online. The neighbor who uses his five minutes of televised fame to tell the world about how terrified he was for his family when the police finally apprehended the criminal who has been quietly hiding in a house only a few streets away, not bothering anyone for the past ten years.

"We could have all been murdered in our beds!"

Yeah. *Those* people. And the screaming woman was a quintessential example.

Her clothing bore not a trace of soot. Her makeup was as pristine as if it had been freshly applied. Yet, there she stood, in the midst of her crippled and dying co-workers, making a fuss as if she was the *only* victim in sight and working my *last* gay nerve. Without further ado, I marched up to her and delivered a healthy slap to one side of her face. Silence descended immediately. Her eyes rolled back into her skull and I caught her before she hit the ground.

One of the paramedics saw what I'd done and looked at me, aghast.

"Best way to deal with hysteria. Didn't they teach you that in ambulance school?" I deftly handed him her limp form.

"Thank God you're here!" He seemed to accept my justification for...er...for *gently admonishing* the civilian as he struggled with his armful of unconscious hysterical woman.

I flexed my chest muscles, knowing how impressive that looked. Besides, he was very good-looking.

"Never fear!" I announced in my deepest and most manly

voice, "the Whirlwind is here!" I know it's hackneyed. Also, as a snarky reporter once pointed out, I ripped it off from Underdog. But one has to say *something* in these situations and, the simpler you keep it, the better.

"How many are still inside?"

He may have looked like a matinee hero but he seemed a bit shell-shocked himself. He nodded and opened his mouth. Closed it again. Opened it. Finally, he just pointed at the ruined building.

"Yes, I see that. It's a building. A burning building. That's falling down. With, you know, *people* still inside? I was wondering if, *maybe*, you knew how many or where they might be trapped? Since you're wearing that nifty uniform and you have that cool walkie-talkie and all."

His only response was to point again.

"You *do* know how lucky you are that you're pretty, right? Because, if you had to rely on..." I tapped my own forehead and sighed, "...you'd be out of luck."

With a theatrical furl of my cape, I left the Good-Looking Brain-Dead Paramedic Guy behind, shouldered through the people still fleeing the lobby, and strode into the building.

Though most of my unusual abilities made their appearance around the time I first discovered hair under my arms, some things are directly attributable to the accident in Travis' lab. I first discovered my weird proximity sense not long after the Whirlwind made his first public appearance. It was while I was helping Gretchen find a kid who had been kidnaped by his deadbeat dad and held for ransom. Her people corralled the perp in a four-story parking structure, but not before the guy had stashed Junior in the trunk of a stolen car. Model parent that he was, he'd also attached a bomb to the kid. Apparently, the police were supposed to back off and let him escape. Otherwise...*kaboom*.

We had no time to go banging on all the car trunks to find the kid, and the computer experts were taking their own sweet time in running the plates of recently stolen vehicles. Cursing the fact that I did *not* have x-ray vision, I ran frantically up and down the rows of vehicles, abundantly conscious of time running out, and praying I'd notice something to clue me in on which trunk hid the kid.

I don't know how to describe what happened other than as a *shift* in my mind. The closest thing like it is when you're jiggling a recalcitrant new key in a door lock. Just when it seems like you're going to have to go back to the hardware store and have them re-cut it, it slides right in and everything clicks the way it's supposed to.

Suddenly, I *knew* where the kid was hidden. I made a beeline for the right car and rescued the little tyke who, incidentally, thanked me by smearing tears and snot all over the front of my costume. The cops relieved me of the little monster, who promptly got *their* uniforms all snotty and wet, and told me that the Bomb Squad was caught in traffic.

Travis could probably have defused the thing in a heartbeat. On the other hand, I'm not mechanical at all. I had a flat tire once and, had I not been able to flag down a pair of lesbians on their way to a folk music festival, I'd *still* be standing helplessly by the side of the road. Having no idea what to do with the bomb, I snatched it up, raced to the roof of the garage, wrapped my body around it... and waited.

In the end, the mission was successful. The poppet was reunited with its mother. The kidnapper was doing ten-to-twenty in the Centerport Penitentiary. Gretchen got some great media coverage out of the thing. Everyone was happy, except for the incarcerated father, of course.

And as for me, I'd just like to say that if you've *never* had half a dozen sticks of dynamite explode between your navel and your groin, it is not something I'd recommend putting on your bucket list. Just because I'm physically indestructible doesn't mean that I don't feel pain as intensely as normal folks. Normally, even a mildly sexy look from my husband turns me on but during the week after the explosion, the slightest stiffening of Little Alec stimulated acute waves of nausea that seemed to start in my balls and settle deep in my stomach. I had to concoct a fib about eating a bad taco to explain to Peter why I had to run to the bathroom and puke every time he touched me.

The first thing I did when I entered the Special Projects

Building was to close my eyes and concentrate. I figured the fifth floor, where the labs were, was where I'd be needed the most. Anyone above that would have made for the roof and, with any luck, the helicopters I'd seen were there to take them to safety, and not just shooting news footage for Yahoo. The floors below would have evacuated to the lobby. But there could be people who had survived the explosion, and were still trapped on five. As my senses expanded, I got the impression of roughly half a dozen pinpoints of varying degrees of fear–ranging from anxiety to outright terror.

In the interests of speed, I ignored the stairwells in favor of the elevator shafts. In less time that it takes to tell, I'd forced the doors open and was standing on top of the car, ready to shimmy up the cable. Looking up, I once again regretted not being able to fly. Superman could have soared through the breach in the wall and flown everyone to safety before the end credits rolled. The Whirlwind was going to have to get though what looked like a scene from the Towering Inferno only forty or fifty feet above where I stood.

I began the climb. The flames wouldn't do me any lasting harm, but I was going to be in agony while I passed through them, so I kept moving as fast as I could. Even worse, I need to breathe just as much as the next guy. Travis doesn't think I can actually drown or suffocate. He says that, instead, my body would shut down and go into a sort of hibernation. Using less scientific and far more embarrassing terminology, I faint. And oxygen is always scarce in the heart of a fire.

This was far from the first time I'd ever been caught in an inferno, but the feeling of being roasted alive is never one that I eagerly embrace. I doggedly gritted my teeth against the sensation of my flesh sizzling while I hauled myself up the cable. Whenever I'm shot, stabbed, lasered, or hit by a falling anvil, I try to respond with a nonchalant "ouch" so that the bad guys know they're outclassed. In this case, once it dawned on me that there was no one around to overhear, I cursed and screamed like a woman in labor. It's surprising how much that helps to reduce the pain.

Once I reached the fifth floor, the leap from the steel cable to the access door was problematic. The angle was awkward and, even under the best of circumstances, my relationship with grace and coordination is tenuous. By a combination of bodily contortions and more cursing, I managed to perch precariously on the minuscule threshold with the shaft yawning below me. It was as much balance as it was luck that kept me from tumbling backwards through the flames and landed on my ass in the lobby again. I wedged my gloved hands into the tiny space between the doors and forced the doors open.

It was like being in that old Kurt Russell movie about the firemen. The instant the aperture was wide enough, a huge blast of superheated air surged into my face. My body was blown backward, across the elevator shaft, and slammed into the far wall hard enough to force every last molecule of air from my lungs and, incidentally, to leave a Whirlwind-sized dent in the concrete. On the plus side, I learned a valuable lesson about casually longing for things like the power of flight. The universe may perversely grant your wish in a way that is highly undesirable. Scrabbling madly, I managed to catch hold of some half-melted conduit, more by chance than by design, and spared myself the humiliation of falling ass over teakettle down five floors.

Once I'd pulled myself through and stood with both legs planted safely, relatively speaking, on the carpeted floor, I needed no sixth sense to figure out where the trapped people were. The screams for help coming from the rest room at the far end of the hall were a veritable beacon.

Bits of things that had fallen from the walls, a few ceiling panels, and some other detritus were aflame in small piles that dotted the hall. The leaves of a lone potted plant and the cushions on a bench against the wall blazed merrily, and there were a few tiny lines of flame chewing across the carpet from one wall to the other where some wiring had come down and was stretched across. But the path to the bathroom was largely clear, and getting to it was a walk in the park compared to what I'd just been through. In seconds, I pushed open the door and leapt into the restroom.

"Never fear!" I proclaimed. "Whirlwind is... Oh, for Christ's sake!"

The scene that greeted me was not encouraging. There were five of them, all dripping wet like puppies that had just climbed out of a sack some miscreant teenager had hurled into the river. One of them, at least, had the smarts to get everyone to douse themselves with water from the sinks before the fire had compromised the plumbing and the taps had run dry. The bedraggled group looked wet, miserable and terrified.

A middle-aged gent with severe burns on one side of his body, was being tended to by a gigantic woman in her late thirties. Melissa McCarthy, before she lost all the weight, looked like an anorexic Gwyneth Paltrow in comparison to this gal, and I did not look forward to the prospect of carrying her to safety. More problematic was the youngish guy who was shaking from head to toe. At first, I thought it was because he was terrified but, when I realized he was in a wheel chair, I figured he must have some type of palsy. The remaining two refugees were a dour-faced older woman, and a twenty-something hipster chick wearing designer knock-offs. The girl looked frightened enough to pass out at any second; the older broad looked annoyed, but I couldn't tell whether it was because she was inconvenienced by the fire, because I wasn't from the Fire Department, or because she was accustomed to being pissed off at the world in general.

I was here but, for once, ingenuity had failed me. I still had no idea how I was going to get them out safely. I had a momentary, cartoon-like vision of myself pitching the fat one out the window to act as a cushion for the others, but I dismissed the notion as uncharitable.

I cast around the bathroom, seeking something helpful, and knowing I probably wouldn't know it even if I saw it. Fortunately, we were on the opposite side of the building from the explosion, so we had a few minutes before things got literally too hot to handle. Before I could finish taking stock of the situation, the Designer Debbie-type decided to take my arrival as permission to freak out. She threw herself at my feet, blubbering "Thank God! Thank God!", and wrapped her arms around the backs of my thighs so that, even if there *was* a path to safety, I wouldn't be able to lead them along it without tripping.

Okay, Alec, I told myself while I thought about how I could effectively take command of the situation. *Deep breathing. Remain calm and centered. Remember, they're civilians and you are a professional. Above all, relax.*

Panic in a crisis does nobody any good. This, I knew. What I did *not* know was what the hell to do next. Recently, Peter and I had seen a re-run of the old *Kung Fu* TV show. David Carradine was always able to get himself out of inescapable predicaments by closing his eyes and using Eastern mysticism to center himself until a solution presented itself. I figured, why not? Then, the minute I shut my eyes, I remembered how Carradine had ended up in real life, and I reconsidered.

First things first, I told myself instead.

I limped to the window with the hipster chick still humping my leg like a randy cocker spaniel. An open window beckoned from the building directly opposite, challenging me to find a way to span the alley. Hands down, the window won the dare. There was no way of getting any of these people across short of chucking them over, one by one, and hoping that my aim was good. Briefly, I entertained thoughts of ripping the plumbing out of the walls and getting everyone to shimmy down the pipes to safety. A second look at my burned, crippled, overweight, hysterical, and/or senile charges and I knew *that* plan was doomed to failure as well.

What I needed was to buy us a few minutes so I could brain storm. I shook my leg a few times to loosen the woman's death-grip, whereupon I began ripping the metal stall partitions out of the floor. I'd stacked several of them against the wall when the older secretary planted herself in my way, with hands on hips, looking at me with arrogant disdain.

"Yes?" I tried not to let my irritation show.

"What are the rest of us supposed to do while you're remodeling the bathroom?"

"We need to give ourselves some extra time to escape."

"You have no idea what you're doing, do you?"

She pursed her lips, shook her head with mock pity and made a grating tsking noise with her tongue.

"I know *exactly* what I'm doing."

During a rescue, it's not uncommon for some idiot to get it

into their head that she knows better than I do. She'll assume that brains and brawn cannot possibly go hand in hand. Since my physical strength is obvious, I must therefore be mentally deficient.

"Pardon me, Mister Sensitive Feelings!" She crossed her arms prissily and continued to glare at me while I stacked the partitions, all the while with one eyebrow cocked as if she was waiting for me to impress her.

"I get it!" she announced with palpable sarcasm. "We'll launch them from the window like flying carpets. We'll just *glide* down to the ground. Imagine that. Prancing around like Aladdin at my age." I ignored her but apparently ignoring her wasn't enough. "No? Maybe we'll drop them strategically so they'll stack up like a house of cards. We'll scamper down to safety like squirrels."

"How about if we cool it with the smart-ass comments, lady?" I swiftly moved the metal panels to the bathroom door and fashioned a ramshackle barricade.

"It's a fire break," I announced triumphantly.

"A fire break." She waited for a long moment before dryly informing everyone within earshot, "We're doomed."

Hipster chick immediately began keening at the top of her lungs.

Whenever possible, one wants to avoid insulting the hapless victims of tragedy who one is trying to rescue. However, one cannot always resist temptation.

"Thanks *ever* so much for helping," I told her with sweet venom. "I don't *need* to be here, you know. I could be home doing something more important. Like scrubbing the rings from my toilet bowl."

The two of us glared at each other while the girl wrapped herself around my ankles again and screamed, "*Ohmigod! Ohmigod! Don't leave us!*"

I thought through and discarded several options, while the older woman continued to frown at me like the explosion was *my* fault. She tapped her foot impatiently until I was tempted to rip off her leg if she didn't stop. Throughout, the girl kept sobbing all over my kneecaps and kept shrieking to high hell. A major migraine started to bloom behind my eyeballs.

I'd had enough.

"Will you *please* shut up!" I grabbed the girl by the collar of her ersatz Dior blouse and hauled her upright. "One more scream, one shriek, one freaking *peep* out of you and I swear... What the hell do *you* want?"

The last was directed at the guy in the wheelchair. He had rolled up beside me unnoticed and was tugging at the edge of my cape. Or maybe he had just taken hold of it. The tugging part could have been caused by the palsy.

"I ju...just th...th...th...thought..."

I bit back my sarcastic quip when I saw the expression on his face and realized that the stammer had nothing to do with his condition. The poor guy was a fan! His eyes were filled with awe at meeting his hero and he was completely tongue-tied. Had we not been on the verge of becoming Krispy Kritters, I'd have bet he'd have been popping wheelies back to his desk to grab something I could autograph.

Seeing his look of admiration and complete trust immediately put my irritation with the crotchety old broad and my annoyance with the Leg Humper into perspective. I was ashamed of myself. No one, not even a superhero, can be expected to be cordial and polite all of the time. All of us have bad days. The thing is, see, in my line of work, almost *all* the days are bad ones. That's what I do. I interfere with *other* people's bad days to make them better.

The fan-boy in the wheelchair reminded me that it was not only petty and self-absorbed, but downright silly, for me to go around resenting civilians because they relied on me to pull their fat out of the fire, in this case, literally. When I take the gifts I've been given for granted, I run the danger of becoming mean spirited. I'm so often confronted with the selfishness, thoughtlessness, and downright stupidity of so many people, all of whom seem to think that I'm *required* to help them, that it's easy to forget that I don't take my marching orders from a magic mirror or a burning bush; I undertook this obligation *voluntarily*.

It was about time I stopped resenting the very path I'd

chosen for myself. I let my gaze wander over the people in the room and I reminded myself that none of them had deliberately decided to be here just so they could get on my nerves and screw up my day. For whatever reason–excess weight, a wheel chair, age, hysteria, or injury–these five hadn't been able to get of the building before the flames cut them off. Fortunately, none of them had been stupid enough to try the elevator.

I blinked as my heretofore under-used brain cells finally kicked in and a new idea blossomed in the fertile soil of my ever-clever mind. I smiled.

"Actually, there *is* something you all can do..."

The heavy girl misunderstood and thought I was smiling at her. Her tears instantly dried, her cheeks turned scarlet and she couldn't look at me straight-on.

Fat chicks and gay guys. It's like iron to magnets.

"I think I saw something in the hall."

"You're not going back out there?" She gasped; her blush faded and she paled at the thought. One hand flew to her overly-ample bosom in a shocked gesture that was surprisingly dainty.

I pointed at the bathroom window. "Get started on breaking that!"

"Listen Mr. Macho..." The secretary actually waggled a finger at me. "You may be all high and mighty, smash through walls for a living, thank you very much. I'm an administrative assistant. Thirty-two years I've been with this company. What are we supposed to use? Our bare hands? Did you think about *that*, Mr. Smarty Pants in the aquamarine cape?"

"It's turquoise," I muttered under my breath. "Wait here," I told the rest in a louder voice. I kicked my stupid fire break aside, spared a small smile each for the large girl and the guy in the wheelchair and exited into the smoke-filled hallway.

"Wait here," I heard the old broad mimicking me. "He thinks maybe we'll rush out to catch a movie?"

To be honest, it was mostly my reluctance to behave badly in front of my two newest fans that stopped me from silencing the old bag's sarcastic comments with a left uppercut to the jaw. Besides, there were other things more demanding of my attention. While I was inside the bathroom, one of the tiny rivulets of flame from the burning wires that I'd so casually leapt over had grown into a full-fledged wall of fire. I tried not to flinch from the pain when I plunged into it and, to my surprise and delight, I discovered that it was barely a foot wide. I emerged in a relatively flame-free area which was nevertheless as hot as hell, and found what I thought I'd seen.

One of those glass-fronted cabinets containing fire equipment hung on the wall. Given how far the fire had progressed, the extinguisher would be about as effective as me peeing to put it out. The hose, however, was another thing. I unwound it, but when I tried to tug it free of its mounting, the unexpected resistance threw me off balance and I ended up on my ass once again. With an angry snarl and a deliberate disregard of childhood warnings that I should "...take that out of your mouth or you'll chip a tooth," I bit into the hose fabric near the coupling and began worrying at it. I managed to get a tear started with my teeth, and I finished by ripping it clean through by hand like I was opening a bag of chips. There was no time to worry about neatness so I draped it clumsily under my arm and around my shoulders and hoped I wouldn't trip over the coils. With my free hand, I grabbed the axe.

Back in the bathroom, I dropped the hose and hefted the axe with a manly, confident grip. Conscious of more adoring gazes from the large girl and the handicapped guy, I squared my shoulders and flexed my arms so that my biceps bulged heroically.

"Never fear," I proclaimed again, relishing the noble tableau I presented. "The Whirlwind is here!"

With a mighty swing, and an audible swish of metal as it cut the air, I slammed the axe blade into the window, expecting the glass to explode dramatically outward.

Anti-climax is a terrible, terrible thing.

The window did, indeed, crack. There was also what one might call, if one were being *very* generous, some shattering in the form of a few minuscule pellets of safety glass which tinkled to the floor. The embedded wire safety screen made sure that most of the window stayed put. With an un-hero-like growl, I tossed aside the axe and punched through the cinder block wall next to the window with both hands. I grunted as I ripped the whole damned window free–frame, safety glass, and all–and flung it into the alley below.

I hopped onto the outside ledge to survey our escape route. Chief Thatcher's people were nothing if not efficient. Either they'd noticed the window popping out of the side of the building or they had heard the crash when it landed. In either case, a couple of them were pointing up at us and shouting. I tried to make out what they were saying but when the newspapers write about "roaring" flame, they aren't being poetic. You never realize, until you're caught in one, just how *loud* a fire in an office building can be. Not only do partitions and things topple over as they burn, but computers and faxes and all of the other equipment tend to explode when they get overheated.

I yelled back but the folks on the ground couldn't hear me either. I suppose we could have played charades. I pointed to the bathroom behind me, held up five fingers to indicate five people, and hoped they understood. I waited long enough to see a fire truck backing around the corner into the alley before I ducked back inside. I uncoiled the hose and tied one end around my middle. Then, I held out the free end and bowed, with a courtier's elan, to the trapped people.

"Your chariot awaits, my friends."

They all looked at me blankly and I heaved a mighty sigh. I honestly don't know what possesses me to try for panache in the middle of an emergency. People just don't appreciate style any more.

"Up onto the sill," I told them. "We're leaving."

"I suppose you expect us to climb? That ledge has got to be five feet off the floor. I'm three years from retirement. Do I look like a mountain goat?"

I was tempted. God *knows* I was tempted. But I kept my mouth shut for once. Instead, I grabbed the stupid cow, and before she knew what was happening, I whipped the end of the hose around her torso a few times and tied it off. Quickly, before she had time for another jibe, I dragged her out onto the ledge.

Below us, the fire truck had gotten hung up at the corner of the alley, too long to make the turn completely. Though the ladder fell short by roughly two stories, it looked fully extended and I figured it was as close as it was ever going to get. Not great, but better than I'd hoped. Two stories is only...what? Twenty, twenty-five feet? Two fire fighters were waiting on the little platform at the top, arms reaching to receive the first refugee.

"You ready, lady?"

Her eyes widened. For the first time, a note of legitimate fear tinged her voice. "You don't expect me to *jump*, do you?"

"Of course not," I reassured her in honied tones.

Then I pushed the bitch off the ledge.

She was in free fall for only a few seconds before the slack ran out and I took the brunt of her weight with my shoulders. In the brief time it took for me to play out the hose and ease her down to the firemen, she impressed me with her vast knowledge of profanity. I learned a few new words that even my days as a street hooker hadn't taught me.

Once she'd been untied and I tugged back the hose, I turned to the rest of my hapless charges.

"You're next."

I motioned to the hipster girl, who was huddled in the corner, quivering.

"Oh, no," she whispered in a high and tight voice. "I couldn't possibly. I'm afraid of heights."

"Listen, sister..." In spite of my earlier resolve to try and be more tolerant, my patience was fading fast. "I don't mean to embarrass you, but all those designer knock-offs you're wearing are cheaply made."

"I am *not*...!"

I cut her indignation short.

"Even if the manufacturer in China bothered to flame proof 'em, it was probably with a fire retardant that does more harm than good. Those things might take longer to burn, but they get very hot and release toxic fumes like nobody's business. If you're lucky, you might pass out before your skin starts to get all black and crispy."

She blanched. A moment later, she was wrapped in fire hose and poised on the sill. Even though I lowered her much more gently and carefully than the first woman, she screamed the whole way down. The instant she reached the platform, she threw herself into the arms of one of the firemen. It was only because I took up the slack in the hose, and because he wrapped his arms around her to save himself, that they both didn't topple off the ladder.

"Me next, please?" This from the large girl. She glanced at the streamers of smoke trickling under the bathroom door, punctuated by a couple of small tongues of flame.

It was the "please" that got me. She was clearly terrified, yet she was still going out of her way to be polite. A hero could learn a lot about bravery from a gal like her.

"Let me get these two out first. Then, how about if you and I go together, girlfriend?"

I winked and she blushed again. It was kind of cute.

"Don't worry," I added, not at all certain, "We've got a few minutes before we're in trouble."

As if to call me a liar, a cinder block abutting the door frame exploded and sent shards flying everywhere. More flames curled through the newly opened gap and started devouring the paint.

"If worse comes to worse..." My mild flirting seemed to have a calming effect on her. "...I'll carry you like a bride across the threshold."

I grabbed up the unconscious burned guy and, as gently as possible, dumped him in the lap of my fan in the wheelchair. The flames seemed to be climbing up the bathroom wall in record time.

"This is the two for one special," I quipped. "You'll want to really, *really* hang on."

He smiled weakly, but his eyes were round and glittering with excitement. He was just as frightened as the others. Except, in his case, there was the added thrill of being saved by his idol; it was clear he'd never dreamed of meeting the Whirlwind in person.

"You ready?"

He nodded and swallowed convulsively.

"Don't look down. Or rather, you can look down if you want, I just don't recommend it. Pretend this is an amusement park ride, and you'll do just fine."

His hands gripped the older man, holding him tightly in place. Just to make sure, I flung a few more loops of hose over the pair to keep them together.

I don't think it occurred to him that he'd be falling freely for a few seconds while I braced myself to counter their weight. Or maybe he was in denial. Or maybe he hadn't wanted to scream in front of me and holding in all that terror was too much for him. In any case, he'd fainted by the time he reached the ladder and it took longer than I would have liked to untie the two of them.

I reeled back the hose.

"Okay, sweetheart. Your turn."

I held out my hand and bowed as if asking her to dance in some old black and white romantic comedy. Notwithstanding the danger, she entered into the spirit of things and curtsied before allowing me to help her clamber up onto the ledge.

"Will it hold?" she asked in a teeny, tiny voice while I fashioned a crude harness out of the hose. "I'm not exactly a size six."

"Me neither, honey," I said with just a hint of a leer.

Her mouth dropped open when she got the point and she flushed. For a second, I thought I might have offended her. But she tittered and shot back.

"Brag, brag, brag."

I couldn't keep from grinning. I didn't know her at all but I liked her spirit. Once I was back in civilian clothes, if I could find an excuse for looking her up, she might be a hoot to grab a drink with.

"Take a minute to relax and brace yourself. You tell me when you're ready and I'll lower you slowly."

She nodded and took some deep breaths.

"Okay."

It wasn't nearly as bad as I'd expected. For most of the way, she went down easier than any of the others. The hose held out until she had almost reached the ladder. When it finally snapped, the firemen had already grabbed her legs so she had only a foot or so to fall. She looked up at me with a little "Oh!"

of dismay while they undid the remnants of my makeshift harness. I watched the realization dawn on her that I would not be exiting the building by the same route.

"I'll be fine!" I yelled. I smiled and waved and displayed my whiter-than-white teeth which are not a perk of my being an uber human as some of the tabloids have claimed, but actually from a home bleaching kit.

I ducked back inside and realized how close I'd cut it. The whole far wall, including the stack of partitions, was engulfed in flame. Burning flecks of paint gyrated crazily on the air currents like tiny sugar plum fairies that some juvenile delinquents had captured, maliciously set alight, and released. Melting plastic dripped down the scorched wallpaper and released a stream of thick black smoke. Had we waited much longer, the scenario I'd painted for the hipster woman would have come to pass. Only my augmented constitution kept me from succumbing to the toxic fumes and, even then, I was coughing hard enough to bruise a lung.

Cursing and hacking, I barged into the furnace that the hallway had become. I stood for a moment, disoriented by the smoke, trying to get my bearings, and swiping at my hair when pieces of burning ceiling fell onto my head. I took a moment to expand my senses to make sure I hadn't missed anyone else trapped in the building. If I had, they were goners; I sensed nothing. Satisfied that I'd done the job as well as it could be done, I took off at a blind run down the hall and dove headfirst through the massive wall of fire. I had some idea landing with a smooth shoulder roll that would bring me right up to the elevator doors.

With all the damned smoke, I misjudged the distance.

Instead of springing to my feet like a Jedi master, I sailed right through the open doors and into the shaft. My hands flailed wildly for another hunk of conduit but luck had deserted me. With nothing to grab, I plummeted back through the raging inferno, twisting and turning all the way.

The roof of the elevator car in the lobby caved in like cardboard when I landed on it. How I was going to explain to Peter why I was limping was something I'd have to deal with when it came up. I shoved aside the shattered plastic sheets of faux wood paneling and warped steel beams and staggered painfully to my feet.

"Do you really want the public to find out you use words like Muthafukinsonuvabitch?"

Gretchen was in uniform. Which meant that slapping her would have been a felony.

"What's the damage?"

Her smirk at my ungainly landing was washed away by a grim fatigue. Normally, Gretchen is overly obvious about being amused by my whole cape-and-costume routine. It's only in times of crises that she takes me seriously.

"Not as bad as it could have been. Outside of those who were killed in the initial explosion, and those poor bastards in the bleachers, very few of the spectators have more than mild injuries. Some of the Greene Genes employees are going to be making nice disability claims thanks to the smoke and toxic shit they inhaled, but not too many are in critical condition. As of right now, as I said, it could have been a lot worse."

"I can tell you there are no stragglers below the fifth floor. Above that, I have no idea."

"And we're it down here," she said, drawing my attention to the fact that all of the stragglers were gone save for her, and a trio of grime-covered firefighters who looked ready to dive back into action in spite of the fact that they were already exhausted.

"By the way, what are you and your buddies doing inside the building?" I asked. "The place is on fire in case you didn't notice."

"Making sure you're okay, believe it or not. When I heard you were trapped on the ledge, I had a feeling you'd come scampering back down the elevator shaft."

"Scampering?"

"I thought I'd spare your feelings."

Shoulder to shoulder, we sloshed through the puddles of inky water pooling on the marble floor and made our way into the courtyard, mindful of cinders from above. My fingers itched to untwist the collar of Gretchen's shirt and wipe a smudge of jelly donut filling from the front of her uniform. Every dry cleaner in town adores Gretchen. How not? Her monthly bill guarantees that all their kids will be able to afford college. The only time you can't use the stains to tell what Centerport's police chief had for breakfast that morning is when she skips meals because she's too busy working on a case, and the crumbs are left over from the day before.

While I was inside, the paramedics and firefighters had been busy. The last of the victims were being loaded into ambulances, and streams of water arched through the air to drench the lower floors. The fire on five was still merrily ablaze but, even as we watched, a hovering helicopter dropped half a lake's worth of water onto the roof.

"Wow!" I couldn't keep the admiration out of my voice. "I thought they only used those things for forest fires."

"Normally, yeah. But Greene Genes has a lot of money."

We walked toward the barricades.

"I'd like to take credit for helping save more people," she shrugged, "but you know how well Jackson Greene takes care of his employees. Great salaries, great benefits and, thank God, a great evacuation plan. They hold fire drills every few months and give prizes to whichever department gets all their people out quickest. As soon as they realized the fire was on five, everyone above it went straight to the roof for evacuation." She frowned and shook her head. "Even so, how many got left behind? A half dozen? More? Shows no matter how well you prepare, something always manages to screw the pooch."

"Tell me about it," I muttered. Then I added briskly, "Well, I'm finished here so I should get going."

"Back to peddling flesh?"

My eyes darted from side to side with no small hint of alarm.

"Relax, Alec. There's no one around to hear."

"Quit it anyway," I grumbled. "Humor me."

"You are *so* touchy. How Peter puts up with you..."

"These tights squish the family jewels and put me in a bad mood. I'm a very nice person when I'm wearing cotton or linen."

"And *such* a queen sometimes." Before I could bristle, she added, "By the way, I hope you didn't plan anything fancy for dinner tonight." With all this going on..." She spread her palms to take in the rubble-strewn courtyard and crushed grandstand. "...I have no idea whether or not I'll be able to make it."

"The roast will keep for another day or two in the fridge," I told her.

"If I can, I'll call you and maybe drop by for a late nosh if that's okay?"

"Just don't expect Beef Wellington."

"Thanks for understanding." She quickly surveyed the surrounding area and, after assuring herself that no one was watching, she rose onto her tiptoes to give me an affectionate peck on the cheek. "Now, go on. Get out of here before you get mauled by the press."

I didn't need to be told twice.

CHAPTER FIVE

"The next time you decide to take a casual stroll through an oven, could you try and remember totake the gloves off first?"

Travis examined the singed gauntlets critically and shook his head.

"Your skin seems to be more resistant to heat than this new compound. Pity. I had such hopes for it. Modified Teflon, an innovative type of asbestos, non-toxic..." His voice deteriorated into an incomprehensible mumble while he continued talking to himself.

"News flash. Fire on bare skin *hurts*."

"Bitch, bitch, bitch."

He reached for an expression that was supposed to be childlike innocence mixed with hurt feelings. Since Travis looked like a cross between Ernest Borgnine and a water buffalo with indigestion, the effect fell flat.

"Here I am, working my fingers to the bone to stay on the very cusp of scientific innovations specifically designed to make *your* life easier, and all you can do is whine when things get a little dicey. This is all experimental stuff, here, I'd like to remind you."

"You're right. I don't deserve you."

He seemed to take my words at face value and deliberated for a long moment.

"Probably not," he agreed.

In a completely just universe, sarcasm would never be trumped by sincerity. Since the universe is unfair, I changed the subject.

"I'm expecting a call from Gretchen."

Travis turned the gloves over and probed at the seams with surprising dexterity for a guy who has fingers like bratwurst.

"She telephoned this afternoon after you went back to the office."

"And...?"

"That is one helluva fine woman." He didn't quite smack his lips.

"Forget it, Travis. She's in love with her husband."

He shrugged with a movement of his shoulders that was strikingly reminiscent of a walrus I'd seen in a National Geographic special.

"Husband's been gone for almost ten years."

"She's still in love with him. What did she want?"

Travis delights in playing stupid sometimes. He's not, but he gets a kick out of misleading people.

The silence dragged on while he examined the charcoal-stained gauntlets minutely. From experience, I knew that if I revealed the slightest impatience, he was quite capable of delaying even longer. He claims that patience builds character. The truth is simpler; he likes making me wait. Given that the subject of our conversation was Gretchen, he was quite capable of a twenty-minute soliloquy praising her womanly attributes. As a gay man, it wasn't something I was particularly interested in hearing about.

"The explosion at Greene Genes..." He spoke just as I was about to snatch up the nearest reinforced metal, super-sonic, ultra-whatever thing-gummy from his work bench and brain him with it. "The fire department is pretty sure it was arson."

That revelation sure as hell took the breath out of me.

"The thing was set?"

"That's what arson usually means. Hey, lookit that! Super strong *and* super smart."

I ignored him. Often, when the Whirlwind is about to embark on one of his adventures, I get a distinctive tingling sensation at the base of my spine. I mentioned it to Travis once but his hypothesis about the cause was pretty crude so I never brought the subject up again. I don't think it has anything to do with my powers or abilities. I think it's simply my subconscious picking up on things that my conscious mind overlooks. The result is a weird combination of excitement and an impending sense of doom.

Most often, that feeling presages the appearance of some new costumed kook who fancies themselves the ultimate in supervillains. Whether it's our balmy weather, the plethora of museums and cultural venues, the general friendliness of our citizens, or an as-yet-undiscovered cosmic convergence of forces deep in the bedrock below Monroe Park, the crazier the bad guy, the more likely he or she will find their way to Centerport. In this case, my instincts were already clamoring that the arson was part of some bigger plot germinating in the twisted mind of a former foe or, possibly, a brand-new arch villain.

I must have smiled because Travis had to fight against a grin of his own.

"Got your attention now, eh Alec?"

Just like any profession, being a hero has its ups and downs. In spite of the constant battle to remind myself that civilians generally don't deliberately get into trouble to piss me off, in those weeks where the only things the Whirlwind does is stop drunk drivers from plowing through schoolyards, and rescue stupid teenagers who climb electric towers on a dare, I go out of my mind with boredom. Boredom, as Gretchen would happily tell anyone who asked, makes the Whirlwind even grumpier than usual.

Ah! But when a supervillain comes along, *I love it!*

I'm perfectly aware that a bad guy showing up usually goes hand in hand with a lot of death and destruction. I certainly don't mean to dismiss any of the carnage as trivial. Unfortunately, the mere existence of a supervillain virtually guarantees that someone is going to get hurt. With that as a given, is it so terrible that I *enjoy* pitting my talents and skills against their machinations and delusions? Besides, it's a public service. How many normal people would willingly subject themselves to the sex-starved psychosis of a mutated mermaid like Erica the Eel, or risk being disintegrated by one of Professor Apocalypse's contraptions?

Then again, I'm not normal. Not by any means.

My parents were Born Again cultists. Though they believed that alcohol was a deadly sin, they had no problem owning a nightclub like Ale Mary's so long as they assuaged their guilt by sending a percentage of the profits back to their snake-handling "minister" down south who, presumably, used the money to purchase bigger snakes. They never really recovered from having brought a faggot into the world. Worse, their cockamamie church taught that it was possible to drive away the "gay demons" by physical and often violent means. Had it not been for my augmented constitution, my body would be covered with scars. Had it not been for my parents hiring an eccentric and brilliant handyman named Travis, my psyche would have been in the same condition. In his own gruff, grizzly bear fashion, Travis saw that I grew up with a strong moral sense and a commitment to using my gifts for the purposes of good. Had it not been for him, I might very well have ended up dressed as a sea captain or a salamander and robbing banks.

I literally rubbed my hands together, eager to get to work.

"First things first. I need you to find out if any of Centerport's usual Parade of Horribles have recently gotten out of jail or escaped from whatever mental institution they've been in."

Travis handed me a print-out. I knew he expected me to be impressed that he'd anticipated my request, but he looked entirely too pleased with himself so I said nothing. I felt my frown deepening as I scanned the list. I even shuddered with disgust when I saw one of the names.

"The Aphid? I thought he was deported."

"Check the notes at the bottom. A few months after we shipped him back to Borneo, the authorities lost track of him. I really, *really* hope he's got nothing to do with this. That sticky goo he spits..." He made gagging noises. "The memory of what it was like to scrub that crap out of your costume makes me want to spew."

"How about Destructo?"

He considered the suggestion for a moment before shaking his head. "Arson isn't his style. He'd have torn apart the whole building by hand. Besides, from what I hear, they got the lobotomy right this time. He's supposed to be as gentle as a kitten now. Works in a landscape supply place over on Parsons Boulevard. I guess if you need to hire someone to move fully grown trees around..."

"Are *any* of these names on here going to be helpful?"

"Nope."

"Then why did you bother...?"

"Because I knew you were gonna ask."

I tossed the list aside and discovered that paper flutters. No matter how much force you put into throwing it away in order to make the point that the information it contains is useless, it mocks you by drifting gently to the ground.

"Okay, Einstein, where the hell do *you* suggest we start?"

He made a great show of scratching his head to indicate deeply profound thinking. Since Travis is a pretty hairy guy, it looked like he was rooting for fleas.

"I think," he said slowly, as if he knew what my reaction would be which, of course, he did, "we should wait for Gretchen to question Peter."

"Peter?"

"Don't fly off the handle. Think about it. Who knows more about the inner workings of Greene Genes than Peter does? This lab explosion..." He shook his shaggy head. "Something's not right. It's only a gut feeling but..." He patted his rather prominent stomach. "...I got a pretty big gut to trust. Then again, it *could* be something as mundane as corporate espionage. There's no law that says stuff like this is *always* part of someone's master plan for something horrible."

"But you don't think so."

He shook his head. "No, I don't. But even assuming I'm wrong, I can still only think of three reasons to destroy that particular lab."

"A fanatic," I said. "Someone with a higher cause who thinks that mayhem is okay so long as they're saving the world."

Travis nodded and looked impressed. "That wouldn't have been *my* first choice but, you're right. I was thinking more along the lines of stifling the competition. Edison used to do that to Tesla all the time."

"The guy who invented electricity?"

Travis sighed. "He didn't *invent* electricity, Alec. Honestly, sometimes I wonder how you figure out which way to turn the doorknob when you want to leave the house."

"You *know* that's not what I meant."

"To cover up another crime," Travis continued. "Arson is great for that. You can steal information with no one the wiser because they think it's destroyed. You can conceal embezzlement. You can even cover up a murder. My money's on something like that."

I was still smarting from the doorknob comment when I saw an opportunity to show Travis that I was far from an ignoramus.

"There's one problem with your theories. The only thing–well, the major thing–happening on the fifth floor is Feed the World. Nothing to steal. No money to embezzle. I can't speak to murder of course but blowing up a building seems like overkill, doesn't it? I'll also bet we can rule out a crime of passion. They were lab techs. I doubt there was a single paid-up gym membership on the whole floor."

"You haven't by any chance heard anyone use the word 'shallow' around you recently, have you?"

I motioned brusquely for Travis to be quiet while I pursued a thought.

I've often wished for a photographic memory. How cool would it be to read something once and have the information at your fingertips forever? Sadly, that's not one of my skills. The only reason I knew anything at all about Feed the World was because it was one of Pete's pet projects. The details had featured prominently, if obscurely, in many of our conversations at dinner when he was unwinding after work. If I had a photographic memory, I could have dazzled Travis with my intimate knowledge of every detail or, at the very least, I could have repeated enough of the scientific mumbo jumbo to make him think I knew what it all meant.

But my husband has very green eyes with just enough hazel to make them look olive, and they sparkle when he gets excited about something, which makes it difficult for me to concentrate. Peter will start in about some new drug that will cure a rare tropical disease, or a test that's supposed to make toe fungus a thing of the past. The more enthusiastic he gets, the more he seems to glow. The more he glows, the better he looks. The better he looks, the more I get this tingly feeling in my stomach and a twitchy feeling below the waist. These involuntary responses make it very difficult for me to focus on whatever it is he's talking about.

Once again, the thought of Peter being mixed up with anything remotely dangerous did not sit well with me

"Travis, you know I have only one rule when it comes to the Whirlwind..."

"No cowls."

"*Two* rules then. We keep Peter out of it."

"I'm sorry but no can do." To his credit, he actually did look sorry. "It's his company. Don't worry. Gretchen's probably going to want to interview all of the executives so Peter will just be one in the crowd. Nothing can connect him with you–with the Whirlwind, I mean. Besides, to a hammer, everything looks like a nail, right? Maybe Gretchen's wrong and this explosion was just an accident after all."

He shrugged but it was clear he didn't really believe what he was saying.

"Some intern could have accidentally started the whole thing by spilling coffee onto a hunk of potassium. It'd look exactly like arson. I did that once in high school. Singed my eyebrows off. I looked like a carnival freak for a couple of months. Come to think of it, that was the last straw before they expelled me." His brow furrowed as he tried to remember. "Or was it that thing that happened in the metal shop?"

It didn't make me any less uneasy when Travis reassured me that Peter's involvement would be minimal. The thought of Peter being anywhere near a situation that might require the Whirlwind to make an appearance, caused the butterflies fluttering around my gut to collide in panic. Most of the time, I'm in complete command of my life. Though Randy *thinks* he runs the agency, when he screws up, he always looks to me to take over and fix things. And I do. But when it comes to Peter, I'm a complete marshmallow.

The minute he comes home from work, even though we've

only been apart for eight hours, my knees go all googly. When we get into bed each night, I marvel at my good fortune in slipping beneath the same sheets as this amazingly beautiful man. Nor am I talking about mere physical beauty, though Pete certainly has *that* in abundance! He's a beautiful person inside as well. I *know* what a terribly flawed person *I* am. It's a mark of Peter's wonderfulness, not mine, that lets him see past all that and still care for me.

He also shows it better than I do. Though I consider myself a romantic, I have to admit that I'm lousy at the heartfelt stuff. Not Pete. Every so often, he surprises me with a little gold foil box of marzipan. It's my favorite, but I never eat it for fear of having to crowbar myself into a size thirty-two jeans. Pete claims he'd love me even if disaster overtook me and I developed love handles. I know it's sappy but, when it comes to my feelings for Peter, even the most saccharine of Hallmark sentiments seem profound.

"If he gets mixed up in this," Travis went on, "I'll do whatever I have to do to protect him. I swear."

I sank into a chair, glum and more than a bit anxious. For once, I didn't have the emotional strength for a smart-ass comment or clever quip. I knew what I looked like. I could feel the tears brimming, filling my eye sockets and threatening to spill over.

"If anything–*anything*!–were to happen to him, Trav..."

Momma Deadly. The Green Gecko. Captain Dirigible. The thought of Peter even being in the same *room* with any of them made my skin crawl. My mind balked at what could happen to him should any of them uncover my secret identity. I dashed aside the tears with the back of my hand. My macabre fears penetrated deeper; my feeble attempts to maintain my dignity proved useless; I started to sob in earnest.

"Aw, come on Alec. You know I can't stand to see you cry. Where's that plucky kid I raised? You know the one I mean. Remember when you first left home and ran into that street gang?"

I nodded through the sniffles.

"They had bottles and knives and lord knows what else..."

"Chains," I sniffed.

"Exactly!" Travis practically crowed. "You see that? They had *chains*. What did *you* have? Nothing other than your wits and a bitchy attitude."

Actually, I had quite a bit more going for me. But I rather liked the picture Travis was painting of me as the valiant underdog and I didn't want to ruin it.

"We're talking about Pete. Where Peter's concerned, I'm not at all brave."

I felt his hand on my shoulder and a reassuring squeeze from his thick, calloused fingers.

"Yeah, Alec. You are." He sighed. "You can be a complete asshole when you're trying to be the Bitch Queen of the Universe, but your soul's always been in the right place. Whatever you are, whatever else you might be..." He grunted with the effort of kneeling in front of me so he could place his hand over my heart. "...You're brave. In here. Where it counts."

"Aw shit." I wondered if my nose was actually running or if it just felt like it was. "Am I gonna have to embarrass myself by giving you a big sloppy kiss now?"

Travis grinned. "If Gretchen Thatcher were to make that offer, I'd *definitely* take her up on it."

"Pig." There wasn't much emphasis to the comment.

"I prefer to think of myself as a wild boar. All that brutal strength and raw power. Not to mention the aphrodisiac properties of animal musk."

"I don't think..."

I picked up a swatch of material from his workbench and blew my nose into it. Travis frowned. I think I'd snotted up a scrap of some amazing new polymer he was working on for the cape.

"...I don't think wild boars actually *have* musk, Trav."

"It's the thought that counts," he assured me.

He stood and took the makeshift handkerchief from me. He held it gingerly with his fingertips and scowled.

"For the moment, let's see how far Gretchen gets. If something mundane's behind the explosion, she'll be able to get to the bottom of it without your help."

"But you don't really think so, do you?"

"No." He shook his head. "I don't."

CHAPTER SIX

The chain clanked and the shackle tugged at his ankle.

Dr. Bradley Harmon cursed aloud. Without missing a step, he reversed course and paced in the opposite direction. At this rate, he thought bitterly, it was only a matter of a few centuries before he wore grooves in the stone floor.

He knew he *never* should have succumbed to Jackson's insistence that he take a vacation! Not after successfully putting it off for twenty-five years, and especially not when he was so close to solving the Three-Two-Three problem. But Jackson had made a good argument for Bradley to use the week in Tahiti to relax and cleanse his mind, if only to examine the problem from a fresh angle when he returned. Against his better judgement, Harmon had agreed...and just *look* what it had gotten him into!

Snatched from a beach, trussed up, and bundled into a small plane like the helpless ingenue from some 1930s movie serial and, now, chained up in an uncomfortably dank dungeon by a madman wearing black leather.

And a mask.

He certainly couldn't forget that grotesque mask. At night when he was huddled under the thin blanket, when his exhaustion finally triumphed over the unforgiving metal shelf that served as a bed, he had nightmares about the thing. As bad as the dreams were, there was something even creepier about coming face-to-face with Thanatos when he delivered Brad's meals. Even worse was the way the fiend stood silently and ominously by the door, his mere presence urging Brad to work faster.

But a process like this could not be rushed. Though Thanatos was clearly no geneticist, he'd evidently taken the time to familiarize himself with the fundamentals of the science. Worse, he had a frightening, if incomplete, understanding of how the Three-Two-Three variant worked, and he was abundantly aware of what it could do.

When Thanatos informed Brad that he would be working on a more effective distribution system for the virus, the scientist had initially refused. Thanatos had accepted Bradley's decision with surprising equanimity. He'd simply attached the chains and left him to shiver and weep in the dark chamber. Within a few hours, the shaking started, followed by feverish sweating, a terrible headache, and increasing weakness. A few minutes examination of his own blood under the microscope that Thanatos had thoughtfully included with the rest of the lab equipment was enough to reveal the cause. He'd been poisoned!

The compound was a fairly simple one, easily neutralized had Bradley been able to get his hands on the requisite drugs. But the chafing of the iron band around his ankle served as a constant reminder that anything he could use to ease his plight was stored in the steel cabinet at the far end of his prison. Not only was it beyond the reach of his chains, but his captor kept it securely locked whenever Harmon was left alone to work. Late at night, after he was securely bolted to his cot in the corner of the room, he dreamed about its contents. It might even contain chemicals he could use to concoct something to eat through these damnable chains and escape.

Harmon would have liked to have put up a fierce resistance. He imagined himself a hero who would laugh in the monster's face or dash a glass beaker to smithereens at his feet with an air of defiance. But courage was not one of his virtues. With the toxins painfully eating away at him from the inside out, he'd collapsed into a pathetic heap on the floor, begging for the antidote through a mask of tears and snot. In return, he promised to do whatever Thanatos wanted.

Later, after Thanatos had allowed him to administer the serum, Brad toyed with the idea of delaying things. There were always subtle ways of botching experiments or contriving to adulterate essential elements. But Thanatos had anticipated that course of action as well. He made it quite clear to Dr. Harmon that the relief was only temporary; the poisons in his system had merely been slowed, not eliminated. Should Harmon seek to sabotage his own work, Thanatos would merely refuse to provide the medicine and allow the poisons to run their painful and ultimately deadly course.

In the meantime, Bradley resigned himself to working, eating, and sleeping in a prison that looked like the set of a Hammer horror film. Deep underground, the stone blocks sweated rank moisture and not even the overhead florescent lighting could fully dispel the gloom that crept into the corners. Though the large space heaters were working overtime to raise the temperature to comfortable levels, a persistent chill lingered in the air. And while Bradley appreciated how the lower temperature was beneficial for the cultures, the cold and the damp were playing hell with his joints.

Thanatos. The ancient Greek personification of death. How appropriate.

There was no irony in the thought, only a deep foreboding.

The original Feed the World virus had been designed to augment mundane crops to heretofore unimaginable levels. Once it was introduced into a host species of flora, the yield from a single plant, both in volume and nutritional value, was sufficient to maintain a small family for days at a time. Even better, the modified plants were self-seeding, and could produce edible fruit and vegetables even in poor soil and under harsh environmental conditions. Thanks to Jackson Greene's vision and Bradley Harmon's scientific genius, hunger was very close to becoming a curable condition.

Until the Three-Two-Three variant showed up.

Somehow, the genetic coding of Three-Two-Three had worked itself deeply into the Feed the World virus genotype and taken root. As a practical matter, the results were deadly. Put simply, Three-Two-Three stimulated the virus to go haywire, replicating madly within the host organism. After a few days of mild flu-like symptoms, any higher life form that consumed fruits, vegetables, or grains infected with Three-Two-Three would find itself altered on a fundamental genetic level.

No longer would the host organism be able to extract or absorb nutrition from mundane crops. The host's body would begin to cannibalize itself at an accelerated rate, desperate to leach needed nutrients from its own tissues and cells.

The only way to stop the process and avoid starvation was to continue ingesting Three-Two-Three tainted foods.

Harmon had worked for *years* to develop a work-around to the Three-Two-Three variant. Just when he thought he'd made a break-through, this madman in the disturbing mask had shown up to ruin everything. Worse, Thanatos had forced him to pollute his beloved Feed the World virus even more. Knowing that the antidote was his reward did not lessen the self-loathing that overtook him for what he had to do to get it.

The steel door scraped against the stone floor, sharp and discordant. Dr. Harmon cringed at the sound. Thanatos' heels clicked briskly as he strode down the stairs and halted at the chamber's threshold. He stood, with arms folded across his chest, and Bradley was fairly sure the fiend was conscious of the symbolism inherent in his blocking the only exit.

"You have news for me?"

There was an odd echo in the deep voice; Bradley had noticed it right away. It was an unusual enough phenomenon to pique his curiosity in spite of his fear. In the wake of their first meeting, the scientist had tried and failed to duplicate the effect with his own voice and had concluded that there was a distortion mechanism hidden within the ebony cowl that covered Thanatos' face from forehead to upper lip.

His captor was not tall, but the skin-tight ebony costume suggested an imposing physique, one that Bradley, conscious of his own pear-shaped body, enviously ascribed to body armor, even though he was half-convinced it was natural. The cape, floor length and glistening, looked as if it was made of velvet saturated in crude oil and Brad suspected that Thanatos was well aware of the dramatic effect it had when it flared behind him. Finally, there was the grotesque mask. Of deepest obsidian, it was sculpted into the visage of a horrible monster, halfway between a skinless skull and the face of a demon from Hell.

The costume covered the fiend's body entirely from head

to toe except for a small ring of skin left bare around the eyes, doubtless so as not to obscure his vision. Even then, the flesh was covered with heavy black make-up which so distorted the color of Thanatos' eyes that, in the unlikely event that Bradley ever escaped, he would be unable to tell the police whether they were green or blue.

Thanatos took a step toward him. Harmon tried not to cringe at his captor's approach and failed miserably.

"Where is it?"

Wordlessly, Harmon pointed to a corked beaker resting in the cooling unit next to the microscope. Thanatos reached for it eagerly. Artificial talons decorated the end of each gloved fingertip. Though they looked sharp enough to slice open skin, Thanatos wielded them gingerly enough to handle the glass container smoothly and without the slightest scratch. He held it up to the light and admired the swirls of golden liquid sloshing against the sides.

"Excellent. Most excellent. I assume this is everything I asked for? Any attempt to deceive me would make me very unhappy. You wouldn't want me to be unhappy, would you Doctor Harmon?"

"Please," Bradley begged. It was a little early for his usual dose but the mere knowledge of the contaminant's presence in his body threatened to push him over the edge into panic. "I need the antidote."

Thanatos laughed. It was a low baritone emanating from deep within his chest, not at all the evil cackle the doctor always expected. He crossed to the steel cabinet, unlocked it, and selected a vial. To his credit, he did not taunt the doctor with it but simply handed it over. Harmon quickly prepared a syringe and sighed with relief as he depressed the plunger. In his mind's eye, the toxins in his bloodstream fled before its potency.

"Trust is a marvelous thing, is it not? I trust you to do exactly as I say. In return, you trust me to continue letting you live. But if the new formula does *not* work as I expect it too..."

Those horrid, wickedly sharp talons adroitly plucked the empty needle from Brad's fingers and dropped it on the floor.

Thanatos lifted his heavy black boot and poised it over the syringe. His heel descended and crushed the glass tube to powder. It emphasized the masked man's point in a way that no words could have done.

"I can't..." Bradley managed to croak past a throat gone suddenly dry. "I can't guarantee how long the virus will remain virulent outside of a host. You understand that, right?" Sweat gleamed on the doctor's forehead; had the room been warmer, his glasses might have fogged with it.

Thanatos affected dismay. "Are you accusing me of being unfair, Doctor Harmon? You hurt my feelings!"

"I won't be blamed..."

"Of course not." A note of sly malice crept into his voice, belying his next words. "Besides, I believe I owe you an apology."

"An...apology?" Whatever Harmon may have expected, this was not it.

Thanatos nodded. "I confess to having misled you. I've made some minor alterations to my initial plans that I thought I should keep to myself. Until now."

"Alterations?" Bradley snapped.

That Thanatos might have dared tamper with *his* creation offended Bradley's ego just enough to overcome his fear and piss him off. Feed the World had been his personal pet project for a very long time and he found it intolerable that anyone would make changes to it without telling him first.

"What kind of alterations? This is *my* project and I will *not* stand for it being tinkered with by some skull-faced flying monkey who..."

His words ceased abruptly when he realized how dangerous it was to let his anger get the better of him. Instead of being angry, the man in black seemed amused.

"You can relax, Dr. Harmon. I haven't touched your virus itself. The changes I made were to the delivery system."

"Nonsense," Harmon retorted sharply. "It's already the ideal system. Messing with it is, quite frankly, stupid. All Feed the World plants self-propagate. Introducing the virus to the original seeds is not only the best way to distribute it, it's the *only* way. I may have no choice about being your prisoner but I'll be damned if I stay quiet and listen to you insult..."

Thanatos held up his hands in mock surrender.

"Doctor, doctor...please, calm yourself. It seems I owe you another apology for giving you the wrong impression yet again."

"I should hope so!"

"You're quite correct. The existing delivery system is already perfect...*if* I intended to infect *plants*."

"Don't be an idiot."

Against his better judgement, Harmon felt his temper rise even more. Though he was a fairly weak-willed man in areas of his life, anyone who questioned his judgement in scientific matters risked a tongue lashing at the very least. Many a graduate student or lab tech had been unpleasantly surprised at the discovery that the mild-mannered, if slightly haughty, scientist was capable of throwing a tantrum like the worst opera diva if he felt his work had been compromised.

"What the hell else would you use it on? Rocks? Animals? That's the damned problem with Three-Two-Three in the first place. The deleterious effects it has on non-vegetative..."

He stopped, thunderstruck when the reason for the work Thanatos had demanded of him finally sunk in.

"Only a madman would consider..." he whispered. Then, his eyes widened as the full impact hit him. "My God! People will *die*!"

"Only a few. To get what I want, I need to be able to show that I can make good on my threats."

"With only a few centiliters of the stuff?" Harmon scoffed. "You can't possibly hope to manufacture more."

"Don't be silly. Of course I can. I have your notes, your formulas. You may be surprised to find out how I've used your own paranoia against you."

"I am *not* paranoid!"

"No? How often does your staff complain about your refusal to share the bigger picture? Your eccentric secrecy has not endeared you to your colleagues, I can tell you that." He shook his head in mock sadness. "I hate to destroy your illusions about yourself, Dr. Harmon. But I understand that, quite some time ago, someone mounted a laminated picture of you inside of one of the men's room urinals. I'm surprised you never noticed. Then again, you'd *never* stoop to using the staff washroom, would you?"

"That is *outrageous!*"

While Harmon would be the first to agree that he was not particularly chummy with his co-workers, he was furious to hear that they mocked him behind his back. His outrage at the effrontery battled his shock and horror at the rest of what Thanatos had to say.

"It was a simple matter to arrange for one of the smaller labs at Greene Genes to unknowingly start working for me. Production labs are used to doing things in piecework. The elements I need, by themselves, are fairly harmless. It's a case of blind men touching only one small part of the elephant and assuming they know what the entire creature looks like. As a result, I should have a nice little stockpile of the Three-Two-Three variant in my hands by sometime tomorrow."

"Then what? You'll just release it?"

"I'm surprised at you, Doctor Harmon. You're not thinking things through. What good would that do? A man like me needs to prove he's sincere before he issues his demands to the authorities. I have a small demonstration in mind. By coincidence, there are some unrelated experiments scheduled to take place on an abandoned farm a few miles outside of the city. Greene Genes *believes* it will be testing a new environmentally sound pesticide..."

"Jackson will stop you! You'll never be able to trick him into it. That man would die before allowing..."

Thanatos shook his head with mock sadness.

"Since you brought the subject up, I'm afraid there's more bad news. While you were on vacation, Jackson Greene received some sad news from his doctors." He held up one gloved hand to forestall interruptions. "I had nothing to do with it. He's simply ignored his health for too long and things are finally taking their toll."

"I'll bet you're just *thrilled* with that!"

"To be honest," Thanatos said, "I'm not. I have a great deal of admiration for that man and I will deeply regret his loss. He was, no, he *is* a visionary."

"You bet your ass, he is."

Thanatos continued as if he hadn't heard. "Sadly, his days are numbered in, well, days. Weeks at most."

"You think you're so smart. But when I failed to return from Tahiti, *someone* would have noticed and said something."

"Very probably," the man in black agreed. "Unless, of course, no one realizes that you never came back."

"Of course they'll realize it," Harmon said. Then he added, because he was still miffed about his photo in the urinal. "I'm sure they don't dislike me *that* much."

Thanatos affected surprise. "I can't believe you haven't seen the news!" He cast his eyes about the dungeon-like chamber, making a production of searching for something. "Honestly, Doctor! I know what they say about television numbing the brain, but it does have its uses. You really should get one. Some of the news programs can be quite informative."

Without warning, he abandoned all pretense and loomed forward. Bradley Harmon quailed before him.

"The fifth floor labs at the Greene Genes Special Projects Building were destroyed in an explosion this morning. Your senior staff isn't fit for much except fertilizer."

"My God..."

Bradley's shoulders slumped in defeat. Every time he came up with a new straw to grab at, Thanatos seemed to have already wrenched it away. Unwilling to reveal to his captor how close he was to despair, the scientist straightened his back, summoned what little emotional strength he had left, and flung his next words with admirable defiance.

"What about Peter Camry? Jackson's protégée. If no one else finds a way to stop you, he will. Unless you've killed him too."

Thanatos' laughter was even heartier than before. For an instant, Bradley thought the fiend was about to lift the mask to wipe tears from his eyes. He caught his mistake in time to avoid revealing his face.

"No, Doctor. Peter Camry is quite safe. It may surprise you to learn that he fits into my plans very nicely."

"Bullshit! I *know* Peter. He's the very soul of integrity and he shares Jackson's vision as much as I do. If you think for one minute you can corrupt him..."

"Corrupt him? Why would I want to do *that*?"

Thanatos' grin became a veritable leer.

"Rest assured, I can handle young Camry. You just let *me* worry about him."

CHAPTER SEVEN

According to Gretchen, who still thinks of me as somewhat of an overgrown twink, gushing about my husband is only one of my more irritating habits. According to Randy, who knows me mostly as The Boss, it's one of my rare humanizing qualities. Travis, who rarely listens to anything I say anyway, seems to take it in stride.

I guess it all depends on how you look at things.

I ask myself, why shouldn't I gush a little? Before I met Pete, my interpersonal relationships were always a little screwy. My parents were kind of shitty. Travis cares for me, but he always maintains a certain gruff distance. He has no problem with me being gay, but he's never been entirely comfortable with it either. And Gretchen, notwithstanding that she's my best friend, can't resist the opportunity to take potshots at me.

With Peter, things are completely different. He never leaves any doubt that I'm the most important thing in his life. Why that is baffles me. I certainly don't think I deserve it. Even so, he proves it to me in dozens of different ways and, every time he does something sweet, I think I fall even more in love with him.

For instance…

Jackson Greene, who was like a father to Pete, was dying. He'd poured his heart into the Feed the World project for years, and now it was blown to smithereens with no hope of salvage. Powerful people at Greene Genes, people like Herman Starcke, hated Peter for his youth and ambition as much as they loathed him because he was married to another man. Still other executives resented Jackson's humanitarian policies, and knew Peter would follow in the old man's footsteps. For the sake of their own increased profits, they'd do whatever they could to see him out of a job, broke, and on the street. To top things off, a company building was a smoldering ruin and people had been killed. My husband was not only grieving the loss of friends and colleagues, but he now had the threat of lawsuits to look forward to.

It had been a horrible day, one that would have driven many a lesser man to seek therapy.

Yet, how did Peter handle it?

He brought *me* flowers!

We're not talking about a single bouquet of gladiolas–which he knows are my favorites. We're talking about *three dozen* gladiolas in a vase the size of a kiddie pool. A man with smaller biceps would have collapsed just trying to haul the thing up the stairs.

At the last minute, Gretchen called to confirm she would, in fact, be coming over. But it was to be a working meal. In the wake of the disaster, she needed his help going over a bunch of Greene Genes-related stuff. It was also a great way for her to share information with the Whirlwind without compromising either of us. Peter had sparked a lot of gossip when he'd chosen to marry an ex-hooker but, eventually, it quieted down and people started thinking of him as an upstanding citizen once again. Centerport can be a really conservative town in a lot of ways. Gretchen might get away with being friendly with Peter, even with me as his "dirty secret" hiding in the background. Come election time though, some citizens would *not* be sanguine about their chief of police openly hanging out with a male madam. We could get away with having coffee in public from time to time, but I had to be careful about visiting her at the station too often. As for the Whirlwind, so long as everyone thought he and Gretchen were only casual colleagues, she was safe. But if any of the bad guys deduced that we were actually close friends, she could easily become a target.

Since the roast was back in the freezer, I figured that, if we were reduced to having pizza, the least I could do was to make it from scratch. So, I stopped by the Farmer's Market to pick up a bag of flour and some fresh ingredients for toppings. With an ulterior after-dinner motive in mind, I also set up the old massage table from my hooker/masseur days and positioned it strategically close to our bed. I changed the sheets and spritzed the fresh ones with a musk-scented linen spray that was advertised to be packed with pheromones – not that we'd need them!

As soon as Gretchen had finished her after-dinner business with Peter, I planned on shoving her out the door and spending the rest of the evening with my husband splayed on the musk-impregnated sheets like a muscled side of beef while I attended to his every conceivable need. I had in mind a back massage, a foot massage, and some other kinds of massages which he'd enjoy even more. In between the massage and the under-the-cover gymnastics I planned for later, I intended for us to spend a good forty minutes relaxing in the over-sized spa tub we'd installed when we converted the nightclub's former ladies' room into our master bath.

The process of converting the club into useable living space has been a long one. Often, it seems like Peter and I live in a perpetual construction zone. Even so, in retrospect, I'm happy that Travis convinced me to keep the place after my parents died. He'd argued that it was perfect; no one would suspect that the Whirlwind's lair was hidden in an abandoned nightclub that was, in turn, located in an area of slowly gentrifying urban blight. He was right of course. But I sometimes suspect that his advice was motivated by selfishness. Years ago, he'd converted a storage space next to the basement boiler rooms into an apartment for himself. If I'd sold the club, he would have had to move, and Travis was far too lazy to want to pack.

For as long as I could remember, Travis was simply around. Whether he was hauling beer kegs up from the cellar, repairing the deep fryers, or patching leaks in the roof, he was just *there*. Until he took up residence in the basement, he'd lumber off to some nebulous "home" at the end of the work day. I never found out where that was. From the slight fishy smell that used to cling to him in the mornings, I figure it was down by the docks. To this day, passing a fish market makes me feel sentimental.

After my parents were killed, I moved back into the small

apartment above Ale Mary's where I'd spent my childhood. I always intended to update the living quarters, and maybe expand them, but with my attention absorbed by the Archer Agency, I never got around to it. A few months after Peter and I started dating, he asked me to move in with him. Though his apartment in the Greene Genes Corporate Complex was certainly one of the luxury units, it had a sterile, mass-produced, laminated feel to it. The vibe it gave off was far too sterile to imagine it ever feeling like a true home. It took a lot of coaxing on my part to convince Peter to move into the former nightclub. And he was a saint himself during the chaos of the first stages of the renovation. Now, though our surroundings were certainly odd, we couldn't imagine living anywhere else.

Travis happily exchanged the role of eccentric handyman for that of an eccentric relative who lives in the basement. Gretchen, for the first time since her husband died, found that she once again had a family to be part of, and effortlessly slipped into a role that lay somewhere between disapproving aunt and critical older sister. It was an odd, non-traditional set of relationships that seemed to work out quite well for all four of us.

"You guys really need to keep the door locked. It's a cesspool of crime out there, or hadn't you heard?"

Gretchen plopped two six-packs of beer onto the butcher-block counter without bothering to worry that the pizza recipe I was working on called for the garlic to be minced, not pulverized by beer cans.

"Do you know how unsanitary that is? Do you have any idea where those beers have been?"

"Put 'em in the fridge then. You can just wipe the counter if you're so terrified of germs."

"I'm cooking," I said, as if the cleaver in my hand and my Kiss the Chef apron were not obvious enough.

"We're having pizza, right? How does that qualify as cooking? You just pop it into the oven."

"It needs stuff on it," I informed her in my best haughty Julia Child voice. "Otherwise, it's just cheesy tomato bread."

"Pizza *is* cheesy tomato bread, you nit."

I changed the subject.

"I see you dressed in the dark tonight? Or do you still believe that when your clothes get to the bottom of the laundry pile, they're magically clean again?"

As usual, Gretchen was slightly disheveled. One elbow of her faded orange sweater had a small tear, and the collar of the T-shirt peeping out from beneath had seen better days. Other than that, and a few coffee stains, she didn't look *too* bad until you looked down. She was wearing a pair of once-brown slacks that were now a color somewhere between rancid burgundy and medium cow patty.

She saw what I was looking at and said, defensively, "I used too much bleach and they faded. I was trying to dye them back but... Heya Petey!"

My husband entered the kitchen. Gretchen stood on tip toe to give him a peck on the cheek and I felt a flash of envy. Peter had just gotten out of the shower and was wearing nothing but a pair of towels, one loosely cinched around his trim waist and the other draped across his shoulders. Had we been alone, both towels would have been history and his cheek would *not* have been the first place *I* would have kissed.

"Hiya Gretch." Peter snagged a sliver of the green pepper I was slicing and, with a grin, popped it into his mouth. Neither my grunt of protest nor my swipe at his hand with the flat of the knife stopped him from grabbing a second piece.

"Good way to lose a finger," I grumbled.

"I'd still have nine more."

He pressed his chest against my back and demonstrated what he could do with only nine fingers by letting five of them creep down past my waistband. I closed my eyes, leaned back against him and inhaled deeply.

Something about the way Pete smells has always turned me on. I don't know what it is. More pheromones, I suppose. It's a grassy, heathery scent with just a hint of something very "male". Even when he comes home after a heavy workout at the gym, when he should stink to high hell, he never does. His natural smell gets stronger and headier of course, but it never becomes rank or sour. Shortly after we moved in together, I stopped buying scented bath soaps and body sprays. Given the choice between Irish Clean, Cocoa Butter Blast or Sporty Fresh, my preference is for Eau de Pete Naturel.

"Ohhh," Gretchen leered. "D'you guys ever think about installing some webcams? You could make a fortune." She rolled her eyes and waggled one finger at us. "Keep it away from the food prep area, if you please."

"Dinner may be late" I managed to mumble past a mouthful of Peter's tongue.

"It better not be. I'm starving." She snatched up a supermarket circular from the counter, rolled it up and playfully whacked Peter on the head. "Put some ice on your ovaries, Petey. Let's you and me head into the den and get some real work done while the Galloping Gourmet over here…"

"I do *not* gallop!"

"The Mincing Maestro," she continued without breaking stride, "finishes his masterpiece. Go and put a shirt on first, will you? All that beefy male flesh is makin' my female parts flutter."

"Your wish, fair lady, is my command." Peter executed a deep bow and made for the bedroom. He paused in the doorway to call back, "Oh…Gretch?"

"What?"

He playfully dropped the lower towel and we were both treated to a brief, tantalizing glimpse of a naked, perfectly formed bubble-butt before the door swung closed behind him.

"I know he's your husband, Alec. But one of these days…" She sighed with heavy, heavy regret. "How come straight guys are never that good looking?"

I shrugged with a self-satisfied smirk. She plopped herself onto a barstool and followed Pete's lead by snatching up a few uncut black olives–from the bowl, not directly from atop the pizza or I *would* have nailed her with the chopper–and rested her head on her fists.

"I'll wait for you to join us before we get into the heavy stuff. You don't need to be there for the background. I already know most of it but I gotta get it from Pete so it's official. Actually," she continued thoughtfully, "I'm kinda surprised at how well he's handling this. It's a disaster."

"He's not. It's just a mask he wears."

"Something you know about," she quipped.

I shot a pointed glance at the bedroom door.

"Don't worry. He can't hear you."

"Still..."

I violently eviscerated half a red onion to show my disapproval of her mentioning the Whirlwind when Pete was around.

"He's super upset but not showing it. Between the fire and Jackson being so sick, he has a lot of things he needs to take care of. I imagine that most people at Greene Genes are already taking their cues from Peter, even though Jackson's not gone yet. Except Herman and his cronies, of course."

"Starcke?"

"Yeah. Anyone with half a brain can see that he's already started plotting to edge Pete out."

"Have you discussed it with him?"

I waved my spatula as if it was a white flag of surrender.

"We have a rule around here about staying out of each other's work. Pete doesn't tell me how to hire hookers. I don't presume to know how the corporate world works. If he ever asked my advice, I'd give it. But he doesn't. I used to push him to try and get him to dump on me when I saw he was stressed. He just pretends everything is under control until it gets too much for him. He gets short tempered and *then* he feels guilty if he takes it out on me. He vanishes into the study to brood. Trying to cheer him up only starts a fight. In the end, we always work it out. And the make-up sex is spectacular. But if you were me..." I pointed toward the doorway after Peter, "...would *you* risk not being able to spend even a single night next to *that*?"

"You have a point."

She picked up a piece of parsley and began slowly and methodically stripping it down to the stem.

"He does it purely for your benefit, you know."

"What?"

"The whole strong and silent thing. I know you, Alec. I see through the masks you wear and I'm not talking about..." She lowered her voice, and the second onion half was saved from a fate as violent as the first half. "...about Whirlwind. I mean in general."

"Do tell, Madame Freud."

"I'm serious. I've seen you at the agency. Behind the scenes, you're like a hostess at a dinner party, screaming at the kitchen staff to make sure everything's perfect. The ultimate control queen in the midst of chaos. Then, when you step out front to greet your guests, you're like a gay cross between Martha Stewart and James Bond. Cool. Smooth. Suave. No matter what the problem is, you handle it like it's no big deal, smiling the whole time and making it look easy. I hate to tell you this but, you're a lot like your mother was while she was running Mary's."

She held up one hand to stop me from interrupting.

"With Peter though, you become this helpless waif. A love-struck puppy. And *very* ditsy, I might add. Oh, I'm not saying you fake it. Both sides of you are genuine. I can't help noticing that the Whirlwind isn't the only thing you hide from him. You conceal your strength as well. Even when he's under tremendous stress, he shoulders the burden because he thinks you can't handle it. If you want my opinion..."

I didn't. But I was going to have to hear it anyway.

"...You need to let your feelings show more often. Not that you love him. God knows *that's* obvious! Every once in a while, clue him in that he doesn't have to be *quite* so protective. Let him see that you can stand on your own two feet. Maybe if he finds out *he* can lean on *you* for a change, he won't be under so much pressure. Trust me on this."

The chopping knife paused in mid-chop, sparing a sprig of fresh basil this time. For all her needling, Gretchen usually knew what she was talking about.

"I show my feelings," I mumbled, barely loud enough for her to hear.

She shook her head.

"You *repress* them. Did you shed a tear when your folks drove off that bridge?"

"Would *you* have gotten weepy if you had been raised by *my* parents?"

"Maybe not," she conceded. "All I'm saying is that you split all your strength between the agency and the Whirlwind. For a change, consider using it to help Pete get by."

"Better?"

Peter came into the kitchen wearing a green sweater I'd bought him a while back that almost matched his eyes–except that his eyes were prettier. By mutual and silent consent, Gretchen and I abandoned our conversation.

"It's certainly less distracting," she told him. "Come on. We adults have work to do. We can leave the child to make mud pies in the kitchen."

"Extra anchovies on *your* slice, you harridan!" I called after them. "Smelly, disgusting dead fishes! It'll be like eating *lesbians*!"

Gretchen scowled and rolled her eyes as if to ask *What the hell are we going to do with him*? A moment later, she slid the pocket-door closed so that she and my husband could work without interruption.

Gretchen's words echoed while I put the final touches on the pizza and slid it into the oven. I'd never been to therapy. In my situation, trusting an outsider would only lead to trouble. Whenever she started channeling Jiminy Cricket, though, I always put up at least a token resistance for appearances sake; I usually gave her advice the benefit of the doubt. In this case, I felt myself balking at what she's said which, I've learned, was usually a good indicator that she might be right. Realizing that only made me resist it more. The telephone rescued me from any more introspection. It was Randy with some minor crises which had nothing to do with Tressman, thank God. By the time I hung up, the pizza crust was golden brown.

Juggling the pizza, the ring of beer cans and a pile of napkins, I took everything into Peter's little home office, dumped the whole shebang onto the coffee table, and plopped myself onto the floor cross-legged so I could serve.

"What's the verdict?" I slid a piece of pizza onto a napkin and handed it to Gretch. For some reason, pizza never tastes as good on a real plate as it does when it's served on a paper one or, better yet, on a napkin.

"Arson," Peter frowned.

"We sure about that?"

Gretchen nodded. "Definitely an explosive device planted in the lab."

"Could it have been accidental?"

"No," he said. "The first thing I did was to check with our Requisitions Department. There was nothing in that lab that could have gone off with a bang like that. Fire? Sure. Blowing out a wall? No way."

"So, the question is…"

"It's impolite to talk with your mouth full," I told her.

"The question is…" She ignored me, and kept chewing and talking at the same time. "Motive."

"No clues so far?"

Mercifully, she swallowed. "Our experts are good but they're gonna earn their pay with this one. You saw the photos? After everything was blown to hell, when the place burned, it burned *hot*. We're pretty sure we already know who the victims were, but the M.E. is gonna have a tough time figuring out which pieces belong to who. Whatever the perp used to do this, it wasn't anything commonly available. Hopefully, we'll be able to trace it and find out where they got it. Even if it was stolen, we have ways we might be able to track it down. But all this takes time. I'm hoping that, while we're waiting, Pete and I can brain storm something useful."

Peter chewed his pizza thoughtfully. "Corporate espionage was the first thing that sprang to mind. But what if it was something completely unrelated to Greene Genes? Something personal for instance."

"Like…?" I wanted to know.

Peter vaguely waved one hand in the air. "An affair. A jealous spouse. Someone who thought they'd been fired unfairly."

"Blowing up a building seems an extreme response to some biochemists committing adultery, doesn't it?" I asked. "I've met some of the eggheads who work for Greene Genes. I wouldn't describe them as particularly exciting people."

"Alec has a point. I don't think the motive is that mundane."

She made as if to wipe her hands on the arm of the chair, caught my frigid glare, and used a napkin instead. Considering the way that Travis and Gretchen both look like the Dispose-All backfired when they finish eating, I sometimes wonder if they might be a perfect couple after all. Maybe they could get a bulk discount at the local Laundromat.

"Just to be sure, I went over a list of the usual costumed crazies." She shook her head. "I don't think it'll do any good. This explosion lacks style."

"Style?" Peter was dumbfounded. "Since when does a bombing need to have style?"

"You'd be surprised," Gretchen told him. "Most supervillains are compelled to...well, it's like they *sign* their crimes. Some are very deliberate about it. Erica the Eel uses dead fish as her calling cards. With others, it's the *kind* of crime that clues us in. Some specialize in art theft; others won't touch anything other than jewelry. If witnesses report Zoot suits and machine guns, we look in one direction; if someone mentions an antique cannon, we look somewhere else."

"And in this case?" I prompted. If the Whirlwind needed to get involved, the earlier I knew it, the better.

Gretchen shrugged. "Violent Violet was my first thought. Explosives are right up her alley. But it seems she's found religion...again. She joined a convent. One of those places where the women take a vow of silence and raise their own vegetables. She had a disagreement with another nun. No one's sure what it was about. The sister ended up in surgery to remove a bushel of zucchini. Violet's back in the asylum under heavy sedation."

"What about the Whirlwind?" Peter asked.

Gretchen and I stared at him blankly.

"I wasn't suggesting he did the bombing, sillies." Pete looked sheepish for a minute. "I was wondering if you'd talked to him yet. Jackson and I saw him on the news, but he was gone by the time I got there. It's hard to miss all that aqua."

"It's turquoise," I muttered.

"My little decorator." Pete ruffled my hair affectionately.

"I'm just saying, if the guy took that much trouble to put together an outfit like that, the least we can do is get the color right."

"He's pretty hot," Peter teased with an exaggerated leer. "That costume clings to him in all the right places. Besides, that's a pretty big codpiece he wears over the tights."

I started to swat him, realized I had a slice in my hand, and hit him–lightly!–with one of the sofa pillows instead. *If you only knew,* I thought, secretly pleased.

"I keep coming back to industrial espionage," Pete said, somber. "I can think of several of our projects that would bring in a few hundred million if Jackson allowed them to be licensed for what they're really worth."

"I suppose it's possible." Gretchen didn't seem convinced. "But the bombing has that supervillain *feel* to it. Dunno why. Call it instinct."

"Feed the World was supposed to be open-source," Peter continued as if he hadn't heard her. "Once it was perfected, Jackson was adamant about providing the technology to anyone who needed it. A lot of people didn't like that. It nearly gave Herman a stroke when he found out that it was the latest project that Jackson wanted to give away."

"What about Herman?" Gretchen's eyes narrowed with suspicion. "Could he have thwarted your boss so...dramatically? He knows Jackson's ill. Two of the deceased board members were already on his shit list, right?"

"I don't think Herman could have aimed falling pieces of the building at the people who disagreed with him. No, unfortunately Mallory and Jacob were just sitting in the wrong place at the wrong time. Besides, do you know how much it'll cost to repair the damage?"

"But you just said...Greene Genes would make a hundred times that much if they pulled the plug on the charitable projects, and sold the stuff instead."

Peter sighed and shook his head.

"You don't know Herman Starcke like I do. Talk about being penny wise and dollar foolish. Quite literally, he has the first dime he ever earned in a little frame hanging on his office wall. If he was involved in this, he would have found a way to do it with only minimal damage to company property."

It was a shame that we couldn't make a case for Starcke being responsible. I'd have loved to have seen the little prick hung out to dry. But Peter was too ethical a guy to pin blame where it didn't belong. Nevertheless, the sanctimonious shit heel deserved it.

Pete read the emotions from my face.

"I know you don't like him, Alec. He's a difficult man with some unattractive personality traits."

"He's homophobic, cheap, smarmy..."

I ticked the man's sterling qualities off on my fingers, one by one.

"Even if he was capable of seeing the bigger picture like Jackson and I do, I thought he'd have a stroke when he saw the preliminary damage report. One look at his face and it was clear he had nothing to do with the explosion. He was extremely..." A wry grin. "...Distressed."

The strident strains of the Ride of the Valkyries suddenly boomed from somewhere in the vicinity of Gretchen's butt–or it may have been the William Tell Overture.

"Sorry." She fumbled her phone out of her back pocket and flipped it open. "Thatcher here."

As she listened, her eyelids slowly opened wider and wider with surprise. Her jaw followed suit, much faster.

"You gotta be shitting me!" she burst out. "I'm on my way."

"I guess that means I should put the rest of the pizza in the fridge," I said.

"What? What's going on?" Peter demanded.

"That was the Duty Sergeant. A couple of hours ago, someone dropped a flash drive off at the station. With all the commotion today, the detectives *just* got around to taking a look at what was on it. It's a demand. A ransom note. A video, yet."

"On a flash drive? Cool!"

They both frowned at me but I couldn't help being impressed. When the Whirlwind first showed up, which wasn't all that long ago, the bad guys were still clipping ransom notes out of newspapers.

"What are we waiting for?" I began gathering up the soiled paper plates and napkins.

"I suppose you can both can ride in with me."

"There's no need for Alec..." Peter's protest evoked Gretchen's earlier observations about his over-protectiveness.

She sighed.

"You know how he is. If we don't take him with us, we'll get the puppy dog eyes."

I tried to make myself look as much like an adorable cocker spaniel as possible.

"Then, it'll be the whole rejection bit with the hurt feelings."

I sniffled and tried unsuccessfully, to summon a tear.

"And when that doesn't work, he'll just keep calling every five minutes to try and wheedle out of us what he wants to know. We might as well bring him along and spare ourselves the drama-rama. Just make sure he keeps quiet."

"Me? I'm not loud." I spread my hands in a gesture of helplessness and tried to project innocence and quietude. I suspect that I failed miserably.

Peter cocked an eyebrow at Gretch and she read his silent question.

"It's a new one. He calls himself Thanatos."

"That's the Greek god of death, I think," I chimed in.

Just because I was hooking at sixteen did not mean I failed to pay attention in high school. Alec Archer is no dumb bunny.

"This is not shaping up to be a good week."

She'd rarely spoken truer words.

CHAPTER EIGHT

While I am understandably prejudiced in favor of the Whirlwind's costume, I couldn't help envying Thanatos' outfit. Whoever designed it deserved an Oscar.

If you've chosen a career path as a haberdasher to a supervillain, garden variety creativity and talent wouldn't be enough. You'd have to pack a wallop of ingenuity as well. Of course, some clients would be easier than others.

If you were lucky, you might end up creating a wardrobe for someone like Captain Dirigible. Your biggest challenge would be in trying to sew enough gold braid onto his uniform to mollify his colossal ego. But what if the villain you're tailoring for has a weird genetic aberration? You can't ignore the presence of a tail, for example, and hope to get away with it. I suppose you could always strap it down, but that's bound to get uncomfortable. The customer might get pissed and, in that line of work, they won't stop at simply stiffing you for the bill. They're liable to make you into a stiff. Even if your client *looks* normal at first, you run the risk of running head-first into obstacles that would be insurmountable to the ordinary tailor or dressmaker. Momma Deadly's outfits might look like off-the-rack floral print gunny sacks, but the last time I checked, Walmart doesn't weave radiation-proof thread into their cotton/poly blends. I sometimes wondered if there wasn't some half-insane tailor, held captive somewhere by a coalition of supervillains who traded him back and forth between them. I picture him cackling madly while he hacks away at a swatch of otherworldly fabric with a pair of pinking shears, and sweats over an atomic-powered sewing machine to put a neat hem into a pair of Teflon trousers.

Thanatos' costume, though, was different. If it was designed to accommodate some strange ability, you couldn't say by me. Certainly, there was enough leather and armor to hide an extra limb, or some grotesque organ, but if it was there, I couldn't see it. What it had in abundance, however, was style.

The pundits always say that black is flattering. What the pundits conveniently forget to mention is that on certain guys, black tends to accentuate the body's more interesting bulges– especially in the chest and groin area. The molded armor heightened the effect, but even so, the smooth, lithe way Thanatos moved bespoke a natural athlete. With a body like his, I doubted that being bullied in school was what drove him over to the Dark Side.

And that cape! Man, the cape was *cool!* Talk about professional jealousy!

I have no idea what material it was made of; maybe Travis could have figured it out if he could have gotten his hands on a sample. It looked like someone had figured a way to combine liquid tar with silk and weave it into one flowing, billowy mass. Unlike my own cape, which only came to mid-thigh level, mostly to keep me from tripping over it, Thanatos' was not only full length, it was *more* than full length. Each time he took a step, it flared behind him like gigantic raven's wings; when he stood still, it formed a shimmery, inky puddle at his feet. That cape was like a living, breathing special effect. Though it was completely inappropriate under the circumstances, I couldn't help wondering what it would feel like to make love on linens made from the same marvelous stuff.

The only thing that kept Thanatos from being a walking wet dream was the mask.

It was ugly as hell, hideous in fact, halfway between a skinless skull and some kind of grotesque demon. The horns weighed in favor of the demonic, yet there was a suggestion of raw, sinewy muscles around the mouth and across the cheeks that gave the impression that the skin had been flayed from the face of a corpse. While Thanatos definitely had the body of a god, thanks to the mask, he lost a few points on the Hotness Scale.

"Alec! What a surprise! It's great to see you again too, Peter."

As usual, Mayor Richie Banterly's only acknowledgment of Gretchen's presence was an infinitesimal nod in her direction. Richie knows she's one of my best friends so he'd never stoop to a snide comment, or an outright snub, not in front of me anyway. But he can't entirely hide the fact that he doesn't really like her very much. I've broached the subject with him a few times but, so far, he's deftly avoided telling me why. Fortunately, I know how much Richie admires competence in any field, whether it be hustling or law enforcement. So, I'm pretty sure he'd never let his personal feelings affect her job security. Nevertheless, I sometimes worry that, one day, I'll be caught between the two of them and my loyalties might be tested.

Richie's political career had certainly been a boon to his wardrobe. The suit he wore must have cost seven or eight hundred bucks; his Italian leather loafers definitely did not come off a warehouse discount rack. When we first met, he was strictly a T-shirt and jeans kind of guy, and with good reason. Even though he was shorter than average, he had broad shoulders and a rock-hard torso that the tight, simple clothing he preferred only accentuated. He never lacked for trade and, from the few times we messed around *gratis*, I can confirm that Hizzoner, naked at the age of twenty-two, was a pretty damned amazing sight.

Not that there was ever any chance of anything developing between us. Richie's build was a little too beefy for me. In return, I'm too much of a pretty boy type to suit his taste. Besides, I'm White. When he wasn't working, Richie preferred partners from south of the border, like his current lover, Julio. They've been together for quite a while; it's only a matter of time before they tie the knot officially.

"Hiya, Richie. How's the First Lady?"

"Digging somewhere in North Africa. At least he'll be safely out of the way if this new lunatic is for real."

I could never remember what kind of -ologist Julio was. He's mentioned digging up pyramids but, when I asked him about finding mummies and curses, he laughed. Once, I asked him to keep an eye out for a baby T-Rex skull. I wanted one to display on the coffee table in our living room. Julio looked at me queerly enough so that I never brought it up again. On the other hand, last Christmas he gave us a pair of embroidered native robes. They were hideously ugly but the needlework was exquisite. Neither Peter nor I would be caught dead wearing them, but we entertained vague ideas of mounting them as "art" for the wall if we ever got around to it.

"You're looking well, Peter."

"You're not."

Coming from anyone but my husband, the comment might have been rude. But Peter and Richie had been friends for almost as long as Richie and I had, and Richie accurately interpreted it as concern for his welfare.

"Yeah, I know."

The mayor rubbed his eyes tiredly. I saw the beginnings of crow's feet and a hint of frown lines that looked like they might grow into doozies in a few years. I also noticed a slight softness just above his belt buckle, and a bit of a droop to his shoulders. In my mind's eye, I always saw Richie as a hot twenty-something hustler. For the first time, I had a premonition of what he would look like in a few decades. The vision was not a pretty one, and it saddened me.

"You've seen the video. Any idea on who it could be? I assume Greene Genes has made its share of enemies just like any other company. An ex-employee. A competitor. Have you caught any brilliant mad scientists doing unauthorized experiments recently? Is there anything familiar about this guy?"

Peter shrugged.

Richie tried another angle. "How about the threats? Is there any substance to them?"

My husband suddenly looked very uncomfortable and I moved to stand closer to him. It must have come across as defensive, because Richie instantly responded.

"Relax, Alec. No one's accusing either Peter or Greene Genes of doing anything wrong. We simply need to assess the practicality of the threat. Twenty-seven million dollars is a substantial amount of cash, though not nearly as much as some of those other lunatics have demanded. If this Thanatos fellow was someone we knew already, Captain Dirigible for instance, we'd know he was serious. But I can't allow Centerport to become an ATM for every whack job who thinks he can hold us hostage for an easy pay-out. Not unless there's a chance they pose a legitimate threat."

"Last week this crazy broad dropped off a ransom note at the station. She was dressed like a chicken in a rainbow-colored suit," Gretchen chimed in. "Or maybe she was supposed to be a peacock. We never quite managed to figure out what she wanted. It had something to do with banning refined sugar. For all we know, Thanatos is nothing worse than an ex-janitor with a leather fetish."

"*Is* there any substance behind these threats?" Richie asked again.

"Like most of Jackson's projects," Peter began cautiously, "Feed the World is primarily a benevolent program."

"I read the specs your people sent over. You can assume I know the background as well as can be expected for someone who's not a scientist. I don't need the details. I just want to know if this clown is a legitimate concern or merely another wannabe looking for attention."

"Any technology, no matter how well intentioned, can be warped. Look at what happened with nuclear power. I can't pretend to have a definitive answer for you. The only person who would know for certain is Brad Harmon. Sadly, he was killed in the blast."

"Although we don't have a body yet," Gretchen corrected, "and we haven't been able to identify any of the...er...pieces as being...uh...him. The M.E. sure as hell has her job cut out for her. The heat was intense. And they had a lot of weird chemicals sitting around. When it all went to hell, some of the bodies got sort of fused together and..."

Richie gave her a very strange look. It was mostly blank-faced, but one side of his upper lip curled up just a little bit and his skin had taken on an odd tone. I'm not quite sure what was going through his mind at that moment but, whatever it was, Gretchen seemed to understand it. She looked embarrassed and immediately summed up with, "I only mean that we cannot confirm he's one of the casualties. Not yet."

"Knowing Bradley, I can't imagine he's still alive," Peter said. "If he were, wild horses couldn't keep him from rummaging through the rubble to see if he could salvage anything. Bradley was a lot of things, not all of them nice. Compulsive, impatient, rude. Because of that, it's sometimes easy to forget that, in his own way, he was as much of a visionary as Jackson was...er... is."

"That may be," Richie agreed. "The question remains though, is there any chance he's still around somewhere and could still help us out with this..." He waved his hand at the screen where the DVD was paused on a close-up of Thanatos' mask. "... or are we absolutely sure he was one of the victims?"

Peter shrugged.

"We're sure enough that Greene Genes has already authorized death benefits for Brad's sister. You know what Herman Starcke is like. If there was the slightest doubt, he would have chewed off his own hand before writing the check."

"I hardly think we can rely on Herman Starcke to guide this investigation," Gretchen bristled.

"That's not what I meant," Peter told her. "I just meant that it causes Herman physical pain to spend money. Trust me, if there was any argument to be made that Bradley survived, no matter how improbable, he'd have glommed onto it as an excuse not to pay out."

"Fair enough. So, the question remains, do we need to start figuring how much cash the city can come up with on short notice? Or do we risk waiting to see whether this guy's capable of doing some real damage?"

"Why is it always *our* problem?" Gretchen grumbled. "Just once I'd like to see Cincinnati held for ransom. Or some place in New Jersey."

"I think," Pete said, after a long pause, "we should consider taking Thanatos seriously."

Eyebrows rose all around and he hastened to explain.

"The best way to alter genes is with a virus. Whenever you're working with something like that, you're bound to come across harmful mutations. And viruses, by definition, spread. In the wrong hands, in the hands of someone who knows how to tinker..." Peter didn't have to finish in order to make his point.

"I still need something more concrete." Gretchen shook her head. "So far, it sounds to me like the standard shtick. Pay up or everyone dies. I need to be convinced that this guy's not just shooting his mouth off."

Richie nodded in agreement.

Peter sighed. "This is all proprietary technology, you understand. And there are almost always difficulties along the way. Nothing major," he hastened to add at Richie's look of alarm. "But enough to give a clever lawyer a leg up, you understand. You'll all need to promise me that nothing leaves this room. Otherwise, as much as I hate to be an asshole about it, I'm going to insist on a subpoena."

The mayor and the police chief exchanged silent looks. They may not have liked each other much, but Richie and Gretchen had sure as heck learned how to work together.

"Fair enough," Richie said.

"Okay then. The idea behind the Feed the World project was to reverse agricultural damage," Peter began. "For almost a hundred years, we've been sacrificing the nutritional value of our foods so that we can ship it more easily, or so it looks prettier in supermarkets. If we could go back in time and taste a tomato grown in 1920, it wouldn't just taste better, it would be better *for* you. It used to be a slow process, mostly trial and error, to selectively breed plants for the qualities we desired. Once we discovered how to manipulate the genes themselves, in the lab as opposed to in the field, the process sped up astronomically. If you wanted to grow cotton that was resistant to weevils, or a banana that stayed fresh for weeks, you could spend a few months with a couple of petri dishes and a promising virus and..."

"Franken foods," Gretchen said.

Peter nodded. "Initially, Jackson only wanted to reverse the process. To put the nutrients and flavor that we'd bred out of foods back into them, hopefully without sacrificing any of the other advantages. Then, he and Bradley had a better idea."

My husband's eyes were shining. Part of it was his enthusiasm for the project. But a little bit of it was because he'd gotten misty-eyed at the thought that the old man he so admired wouldn't be around for much longer.

"Why not, they thought, create foods that were *healthier* than Nature intended? Not just restore the lost nutrients that we'd bred out, but pack 'em chock full of stuff that was even better for you. Once they set their minds to it, it turned out that it was surprisingly easy to create a virus which more or less did what they wanted."

"More," Richie asked, deadpan, "or less?"

"Exactly," Peter said.

"Tell me about the 'less' part," Richie said.

"I don't understand all of it," Peter confessed. "My expertise is in business, not biology. From what little I do know, the first hurdle was that the new virus spread *too* well. If you planted a single radish, for example, it could infect all the radishes around it. And not just the radishes. The virus could cross species and infect the corn, the wheat, the strawberries..."

"I can see how that would create legal problems for Greene Genes. But if that's all there is to Thanatos' threats, we can tell him to take a hike. Let the Greene Genes lawyers handle the claims from angry farmers. It's none of the city's business."

"I'm afraid there's a little more to it than that, Richie." Peter looked extremely uncomfortable. "First, though, I want to assure you that we scotched this part of the research as *soon* as we realized how dangerous it was. Or, at least, that's what I was told."

We all waited, with varying degrees of impatience.

"There was another glitch with the virus. It wouldn't stop with changing the crops alone. It infected anything that ate the crops. It didn't matter what it was–a cow, a rabbit, a bird, or even a human being. After the virus got into the new host's system, it went to work again. The early symptoms were mild, no worse than a slight cold. But after the host recovered–and I want to make it clear that the hosts *always* recovered, by the way–they lost the ability to absorb nutrition from uninfected food."

"Are you saying," Richie's brow furrowed, "they had to eat the Greene Genes food or...starve?"

Peter nodded. "You can see why we put a stop to it. Onlyit didn't stop."

"Go on."

"A few months ago, out of nowhere, Brad Harmon announced that he'd made a major breakthrough in connection with the Three-Two-Three variant. That's what we called the toxic gene. He claimed he was this close..." Peter held up two fingers. "... to solving all the problems. Naturally, the Board was concerned about the way that he'd continued working in secret. There was even talk about firing him because of it."

"I take it that Jackson Greene stopped it?"

Peter nodded. "He pointed out that, if Bradley had done what he claimed, even if we gave away the new technology for free–which was always Jackson's plan, by the way–Green Genes' stock would *still* go through the roof."

"And your Board agreed to that?"

"Some more reluctantly than others," Peter told him. "But they all came around in the end. At least temporarily. We agreed to delay our final determination until Bradley presented his results to the Board. That was scheduled for a few weeks after he got back from Tahiti. To give him a little extra time to work out the final bugs."

"Wait a minute. Greene Genes let him take a *vacation*?" Gretchen said, with disbelief. "On the verge of a major breakthrough like this?"

Peter chuckled.

"You can bet your asses that Bradley fought them on it. Jackson insisted."

"Doesn't that strike you as odd?"

Peter shook his head. "Not for Jackson, it wasn't. Don't forget, he'd known Brad Harmon for years and years. They're both workaholics, but Jackson handles it better. Bradley, at the best of times, is a walking nerve ending. Jackson knew how much was riding on this project and he wanted Bradley rested and relaxed when he made his presentation to the board. If Brad walked in looking as he usually did, like a half-crazed, over-caffeinated kangaroo, the board would not have been very receptive."

"That makes sense, except..." A thought occurred to

the mayor. "Is it possible that your Doctor Harmon actually *did* have a breakdown and...well...recreated himself as this Thanatos character?"

I giggled. I couldn't help myself. The three of them targeted me with looks ranging from puzzled to irritated.

"Are we talking about the same Dr. Bradley Harmon?" My giggle grew into outright laughter. "Haven't you all met him? It would take a crowbar to get him into that costume. Brad Harmon may want to give the world better nutrition, but I'll bet it's been twenty years since he put anything that actually came out of the ground into his own mouth." I pointed at the image of Thanatos, still frozen on the screen. "Maybe if this guy was calling himself Mister Microwave or The Big Bad Belly."

"Alec's right. We had to hire Bradley a nutritionist after his last physical because he refused to eat properly. He claimed he had no time to worry about it. She almost had a heart attack herself when she found out how long he'd been surviving on coffee, Chinese take-out, and potato chips. I doubt that two weeks on the beach were enough to melt fifty pounds off him and put him in that kind of shape."

"More like seventy-five pounds," I chimed in, just to be helpful.

"I'd feel better if we had a better idea of what the connection was between Greene Genes and this clown," Gretchen said. "He seems to have a vendetta against the company."

"Not to mention a degree of inside knowledge that I find alarming," Richie said. "I don't think it's coincidence that he showed up spouting off about your Feed the World project less than twenty-four hours after the scientists who developed it were blown to hell. By your own admission there were dangers associated with this thing."

"Which we abandoned and took precautions against," Peter quickly reminded him.

"But it could still be weaponized."

"I think that 'weaponized' is a pretty strong term."

"I'm not comfortable with it," Richie decided, cutting off Peter's protest and addressing Gretchen. "I don't think we can afford to dismiss these threats out of hand. Can you get in touch with your friend in the blue cape?"

I bit my tongue.

"I haven't heard from him since the fire this morning. But I'm sure he'll turn up again soon."

"Let me know the minute he does. I'm not looking forward to whatever kind of demonstration this Thanatos fellow is planning during your field tests tomorrow, Peter. What exactly is it you're doing?"

"Nothing that'll result in giant zucchini attacking the city," Peter assured him. "Nothing to do with the Feed the World project. It's a fairly routine test of a new pesticide. We already know it's non-toxic and won't negatively affect the environment. What we need to find out now," Peter grinned, "is whether or not it actually kills the bugs. With all the regulations we have to deal with, that part sometimes gets lost. If we're lucky..."

Richie cut him off with an exclamation that was half grunt and half growl. He used to make that sound sometimes when we were younger when he was telling me about a trick that hadn't gone well. I rarely heard him do it anymore. While it was fine for a hustler on the street, it was a little too animalistic, and not very dignified, coming from an elected official.

"I'm hoping that this creep is nothing but bluster. On the other hand, I remember what happened when we failed to take Professor Apocalypse seriously that first time. So, we're going to proceed as if we're facing a legitimate threat. If it turns out that Thanatos is not much more than a wet dream in black leather..."

It seems I wasn't the only one who'd noticed.

"... the worst that can happen is that we'll all spend a few sleepless nights worrying over nothing."

"If you've no objection, Peter," Gretchen chimed in, "I want to post a few of my officers around your testing site tomorrow."

"You'll do more than that," Richie told her in a tone that brooked no argument. "When I said we're going to treat this a legitimate threat, I meant it. I want a *strong* police presence there. Be on the lookout for even the slightest irregularity. Peter, you make sure the Greene Genes security people are on heightened alert as well. No one gets anywhere near that testing area unless they're authorized by your company or on Gretchen's payroll. I will be quite happy if we *never* find out what Thanatos wanted to demonstrate. Gretchen, if you can get hold of the Whirlwind, I want him put on the alert as well. Oh, and Alec?"

It took me a second to realize the mayor had switched conversational gears.

"If that boy Henry is available tonight, I wanted to send Orin Culpepper a little thank you for his very generous donation to the Fine Arts Museum."

"Have your secretary call Randy and he'll set it up. We'll bill your account." Far be it from me to ever turn down a paying client.

"Good. Keep me posted everyone."

After he left, I stood and wondered what was next until I realized that both Gretchen and Peter were itching to get to work but didn't want to be obvious about throwing me out.

"Well!" I said brightly. "Another day, another dollar. I might as well head home and spend the rest of the evening catching up on paperwork. In the meantime, if anyone needs a distraction, a clever bon mot, or some fashion advice, I'm only a phone call away." I gazed through lowered lashes for Pete's benefit. "Or maybe a lap dance?"

"I love you, Alec. Don't ever forget that." Peter kissed me so deeply that even Gretchen blushed. "Now, get out."

My butt tingled from his affectionate swat as I made my way out of the building. On the way, I telephoned Randy to warn him he'd better be on his best behavior when the Mayor's office called. I also let him know I had some unexpected business to take care of, and he should plan on holding the reins for a few days. Then, I called Travis and told him to stay put until I got home.

He and the Whirlwind had a *lot* to discuss.

CHAPTER NINE

"Genetics is not one of my best areas."

"So, you can kiss the Nobel Prize goodbye. I'll bet you're still more competent than half the scientists out there."

Travis heaved an overblown sigh of contentment, clasped both hands over his heart, and did his best to flutter his eyelashes–which looked very strange as, only a few days ago, one of his experiments had gone wrong and he'd seared off his lashes and his eyebrows.

"Such confidence in my abilities, kiddo. Touches me right here. Now, do yourself a favor and *try* not to move."

"That's easy for *you* to say. It's freezing."

"Don't be such a whiner. It's at least ten degrees above freezing. Celsius."

"Ten degrees," I marveled. "Celsius! Imagine that!"

I was strapped, spread-eagled, to a table in Travis' lab, wearing nothing but a pair of briefs. The metal surface was colder than a witch's you-know-what where it made contact with the bare flesh of my back and shoulders. Even though the skivvies insulated them more than the rest of me, my testicles kept trying to retreat through my stomach and wrap themselves in my intestines for warmth.

Travis had draped me from throat to mid-thigh with a sheet of thin fabric. I was under no illusion that he'd done it for my comfort.

"Can't I put on a shirt at least? Maybe a light sweater? A ski parka?"

"Quiet. I'm multi-tasking."

He waddled over to one of a half dozen computer terminals

and typed something, his fingers moving like sausages on amphetamines.

"Not that I want to distract you further by complaining, but I'd really feel a lot better if you would concentrate on one thing at a time. Especially since I've got this...*thing* that looks suspiciously like a flame-throwing bazooka pointed at my chest. What the hell is it anyway?"

"A flame throwing bazooka."

I tightened my muscles and started to tug at the straps holding me in place before I realized he was joking and relaxed.

"This'll keep your mind off the cold while I'm conducting the test. Lookie here."

The lights dimmed and a holographic projection appeared in mid-air about a foot and a half above my face, and slightly to my right. I blinked a couple of times and my head swam with dizziness. If my hands had been free, I'd have clapped them to my temples to make sure my brain stayed inside my skull.

"Dammit, Trav. You know how much I hate when you do that. If I puke all over myself, won't that screw up your data?"

There was a very good reason why Pete and I never went to 3-D movies. Five minutes into the film, I inevitably made a beeline for the men's room. I don't think it has anything to do with my odd genetics; I think it's plain, ordinary motion sickness. I will concede defeat in a heartbeat to the first supervillain who traps me on one of those spinning, whirling amusement park rides. Even the teacups at Disneyland would probably give me a migraine and make me throw up.

"Take a look at this while we're powering up."

He flicked a switch and the hologram stabilized. My stomach settled a little but the hovering image was still too close to my eyes. A sick headache threatened when I tried to keep it in focus.

"This part is what concerns me most." Part of the diagram where the little hexagons and threads seemed to be more densely crammed together started to glow. "I know better than to try and educate you on the details. So, I'll cut to the chase." He pointed. "The key is right here."

A low beep sounded from a console below my line of sight. Travis moved to fiddle with the dials, and he grunted something incomprehensible. He returned to my side and began fussing with the contraption suspended over my torso.

"I don't mean to be a spoil sport. But it's disconcerting enough to have that thing hanging from the roof, aimed at me, without you fiddling with it. If you break it, it's gonna fall. When it falls, it's gonna fall on me."

With a snort of irritation, he grabbed the thing and, using his full body weight–which was considerable–he gave it a massive tug. I yelped and squeezed my eyes closed, but when I opened them, it was swaying alarmingly but still more or less in place. Even better, the roof of Ale Mary's seemed intact. So far.

"Satisfied? And just FYI, since it's got to be calibrated to the nearest micrometer, you're just gonna have to stay put until it stops swinging and I can adjust it again."

"What exactly are you doing?"

"You wouldn't understand it."

"Since I'm the one strapped to the torture table, I think I have a right to know. Try me."

"Torture table." He rolled his eyes. "You are *such* a drama queen! I'm testing this new material to see how it holds up."

"Against what?"

"The usual stuff. Laser beams. Heat rays. Various kinds of radiation."

"Then what do you need me for?"

He shot me a withering look.

"To see if anything penetrates," he said, in a tone that clearly communicated that he thought it was obvious. "I suppose I could just drape it over a dummy..."

"That sounds like a great idea."

"But nothing beats testing under field conditions, as it were. Are you paying attention to the hologram? *You* asked, remember?"

I bit back a snarky comment and tried not to shiver. I don't really resent when Travis treats me like some kind of guinea pig except when he treats me like...well...some kind of guinea pig. Even guinea pigs have feelings. They also have built in fur coats to insulate themselves from chilly steel tables whereas I have to content myself with my baby soft skin.

"Hey!" Something about the hologram caught my attention. "There's a Greene Genes logo on this picture."

"Huh? I don't know what you're talking about." He ducked below the edge of the table, ostensibly to tighten one of the straps that held me in place. But I nonetheless caught a glimpse of his guilty expression.

"You hacked it again! Dammit, Travis."

"I didn't use Peter's access codes. I swear!"

"You better not have. If he gets fired because of something you did…" I left the threat dangling.

"I used a very sophisticated, very stealthy back-door virus. They'll never know it's there, let alone trace it. This Feed the World project makes for some interesting reading."

"How did you get your hands on it? I thought they lost everything when Dr. Harmon was killed in the explosion. That's what Pete and Gretchen seem to think."

"They're not entirely wrong. The project itself is well-documented and Greene Genes still has most of the data, right up until they backed themselves into a corner. Something called Three-Two-Three. That's what Bradley was working on, and that's what he was so secretive about. Apparently, he used his own laptop for that. None of *that* data is stored on the main frame. Trust me. I looked."

There was little point in my badgering him about it. He knew how I felt about his hacking and he did it anyway. Short of turning him in, there was no way to stop him.

"This is the Feed the World genetic map," he continued. "If Thanatos has made the changes I think he has, the folks at Greene Genes are gonna give me a medal when I hand all of this 'lost' data over to them. Take a gander at this part of the RNA duplication process right here. It just cries out to be altered, dontcha think?"

"Yeah. Sure. It practically screams. Whatever."

Something new on the hologram started glowing. I had no idea what it meant.

"Now, this part here," he explained, "is a flaw in the genotype. Well, maybe that's the wrong word. It's more of a weakness. A susceptibility. This is what Peter was talking about. It's the point where the infection or whatever-it-is threw a monkey wrench into the works."

He suddenly looked very grave.

"The notes I found refer to it as Three-Two-Three. I guess that's some kind of batch number or experimental lot. Whatever number you wanna give it, it's a mutation that affects the very genes that make the virus do they very things they designed it to do."

His fingers whipped across the keyboard and made the floating image blur and shift. I closed my eyes again.

"Could you please not do that? I'm nauseous enough already."

"Fine." He shrugged. "If you don't want to know, and you're so anxious to get the experiment started, just focus your attention here instead." He wheeled over a cart with a monitor on top, and positioned it so that I could easily see the screen. It showed a graph with bars representing about twenty different kinds of data. "If any of these go into the red while I'm re-calibrating, your job is to let me know right away." He tapped the contraption hanging above me with affection. "We just wanna test this little baby today and see if the new fabric blocks the radiation, not turn you into a melted pile of sludge."

The hologram shifted onto its side. My head spun even faster.

"No rush," I said. The longer the contraption above me took to warm up, the happier I'd be. "You can go ahead and finish what you were telling me."

"It looks like they succeeded in creating a virus that really and truly intensifies the nutritional values of food. Had it worked, it wouldn't have been just a new and better food source, it very well could have ended world hunger. Unfortunately, the design is flawed. The little bugaboo continues to alter its environment to guarantee its own survival, even after its initial task is done. The result is a more or less symbiotic relationship."

"You wanna put that in English, Einstein?"

Travis frowned.

"Think of it as a kind of parasite. A cancerous parasite that spreads. Peter wasn't kidding about the consequences. This

Three Two Three stuff is probably the healthiest food on the planet. But the second you try to chow down on normal foods, your body finds itself unable to process the nutrients. In short, you can eat all you want and end up starving to death."

I tried to look like I understood what he was saying. I also tried to look away from the dizzying hologram so I could keep last night's dinner exactly where it was supposed to be. The only other place to look was at the screen atop the little cart.

"Uh, Travis?" I squealed, panic blossoming. "Red. It's turning red. Melted sludge, remember?" I struggled against the straps until I felt his massive paw in the middle of my chest pressing me back onto the table.

"Don't be such a goose, Alec. I know science isn't your thing." He tapped the screen with one finger. "It doesn't matter if *those* turn red. It's the *other* ones we need to watch. Now, where was I?"

More switches got switched; more levers got levered; more toggles got toggled. The machine above me began to hum. It pulsed and made an unexpected and alarming crackling sound, like when you flip a light switch and the bulb is about to blow. I much preferred the gentle hum. I also would have felt a lot better if the end closest to my chest, the part that looked suspiciously like a gun-muzzle, hadn't started glowing quite so brightly.

"This Thanatos goon is talking about immediate and widespread contamination. But that's the part I don't understand. Even with this Three-Two-Three variant, there's bound to be a delay What he's talking about doesn't seem possible."

He paused to put on a pair of very dark, very thick goggles.

"You've got to give the crops time to grow first."

"What's with the goggles?"

"Protection," he shot back perfunctorily. "Are you paying attention to what I'm saying?"

"I'm paying more attention to the fact that *you* have goggles and I didn't get any."

"Don't look directly at the tip and you'll be fine."

"Are you nuts?" There was a definite squeak in my voice now. "How can I *not* look at it? It's got sparks and shit coming out of it! Not that you care, but I'm feeling kinda vulnerable right about now. I'm laying her practically naked while your laser whatsis is revving up to blast me in the chest."

"That's what the polymer fabric is for." He didn't seem terribly concerned.

"It can't keep the freaking chill off the table, Trav. Do you honestly expect it to stand up against that *thing*?"

"That's what we're about to find out!"

The glowing tip grew too bright to look at directly. I made the mistake of looking at the screen next to me instead, and I saw that now *all* of the bars were well into the red zone.

"Holy sh...!!!" I yelled.

There was a deafening *crack!* I felt a red-hot sledge hammer slam into my chest. I half expected the breath that exploded from my lungs to be super-heated steam. I fully expected that pieces of fried gall bladder and spleen were dripping from my nostrils. Every muscle in my body contracted forcefully enough to *propel* sprays of sweat from my pores. Had anyone snapped a photo of me at that instant, I swear to God I would have looked like a fountain in a shopping mall food court.

"Unless of course, he's found a way to spread the virus without bothering to grow the crops first. He might be trying to introduce it directly into the hosts. If that's the case, we could be in for a whole mess of trouble," Travis continued, oblivious to my distress. "I'll bet you a small beer that's his plan. If not, it's got to be something mighty close to it."

"Gurgle, gurgle." I was trying to figure out how, after almost thirty years of not thinking about it, I'd suddenly forgotten how to breathe.

"I tell you, Alec, this situation scares the bejesus outta me. The consequences of releasing this altered bugaboo could be world changing. You okay, kiddo?"

This time my response was a very distinct "growlf," with a couple of "awks" and "acks" thrown in for emphasis.

"Knocked the wind outta ya, huh? Hang on a sec."

An instant later, the numbness in my chest was replaced by an extraordinarily unpleasant feeling in the pit of my stomach. It was a lot like being punched in the stomach by a musk ox wielding an ice axe. It drove out what little air remained in my lungs and, purely by instinct, I gasped and found I was able to breathe again. When my vision cleared, I saw Travis was holding a compressed air cannister that was coated with frost and had wisps of what looked like steam rising from the end of the nozzle.

"Did you just…" I gasped, "…*hit* me with that?"

"Stay put while the computer's tabulating the results. If we're lucky, we won't have to do it again."

"That's just peachy."

"As I was saying…" He tossed the cannister into a corner where it landed with a clang. "If this virus escapes, millions of people could die and yet…" His voice trailed off and he scratched his head. "When I was watching that video, I got the strangest feeling that Thanatos isn't a pro. The guy isn't nearly as grandiose and melodramatic as your typical arch villain is. He strikes me as a newbie. Strictly small time."

"I didn't get the idea he was *small* at all." I managed a weak leer.

"Try thinking with your brain once in a while, Alec. The big one, not the little one."

"I am thinking! To the extent that I can after you *hit* me with a freaking air tank!"

"Not air," he corrected. "Liquid nitro."

"Like that makes a difference?" I struggled more forcefully against my bindings. "I would *really* like to get up now."

"Not just yet."

He whipped away the sheet covering me and inspected it for a long moment. When he was satisfied with whatever he saw, he held it up to show me. He looked like a bearded, glandular preschooler hoping the teacher would coo over his first attempt at finger painting.

"Bee-yoo-ti-ful, ain't it?"

"It's a sheet, Travis. From this angle, I'm not even sure the thread count is higher than 250. What is this nonsense about Thanatos being an amateur terrorist?"

"I can't put my finger on why but I get the impression that he doesn't fully understand the value of what he's got. Either that, or he hasn't thought things through very well. His ransom demand would be pocket change to someone like Momma Deadly."

Travis shook his head again.

"If this mutation is such a big deal, why not ask for a nice round fifty million? Or a hundred? But what does he want? A piddly twenty-seven million. Doesn't it seem strange, almost like he picked the number out of a hat? If we look at the Feed the World virus as the hammer, twenty-seven mill is a pretty small nail. Unless…"

He paused, lost in thought.

"Unless…?" I prompted.

"Unless what we think is a big old sledge hammer is really one of those itty-bitty ones for pounding tack."

"I have *no* idea what the hell you are talking about."

"What if the virus isn't really capable of doing any damage?" he explained without really explaining anything at all.

"When you're finished speaking in tongues…" I shifted my weight from side to side, trying to make the table wiggle. "I'd appreciate it if you could tell me how much longer I need to stay pinioned to this thing."

"Pinioned?" Travis looked amused. "I know you think using fifty cent words make you seem smarter, Alec. But nobody actually uses the word 'pinioned' anymore."

"The Aphid did!"

"The Aphid is a psychotic maniac," he pointed out. "I need to get some control data and then we're done. In the meantime, we can turn this off. That should make you happy."

The hologram vanished. So long as my nausea didn't take its own sweet time following it into oblivion, my day might improve.

"Getting back on topic, what do you mean that the virus might not be dangerous?"

"I'd have thought it was obvious even to someone who uses a word like 'pinioned' in a sentence. Thanatos may not realize that his plan was doomed from the beginning."

I stuck my tongue out at him but he continued unabated.

"According to what I can tell from Bradley Harmon's notes,

it looks like he was very close to finding a solution to the Three-Two-Three problem. He might even have actually done it, though it still remained to be tested. But Thanatos doesn't seem to know that. So, let's assume that he releases the mutated versions of the virus into the world."

"The virus that Bradley fixed?"

Travis shrugged.

"It's possible, isn't it? And, if so, what harm would it do?"

"You just said…"

"All Thanatos will have done would be to carry out Jackson Greene's original vision."

"You're saying that everyone would be eating the genetically altered food." I paused to think through what he was suggesting. "It's much more nutritious. It's easier to grow. It's more resistant to disease. And yadda, yadda, yadda and so on and so forth."

"Exactly!" Even though he picks on me mercilessly, Travis takes genuine delight when I manage to work things out without being prompted. "The irony is, if Thanatos carries out his threat, and if the virus spreads as quickly as we think it could, what would it matter if everyone gets infected with it? All the food would be infected as well. We could truly see an end to world hunger."

"So, you're saying Centerport shouldn't pay the ransom?"

"Do you know how strange it is that I don't actually remember your mother ever dropping you on your head as a child? Now, be still again." He returned to fiddling with his machine.

"Hardy, har, har," I shot back, tonelessly voicing my displeasure.

While I was pretty sure that I'd managed to follow Travis' logic, I wasn't quite as certain that I completely understood what he was getting at. Ending world hunger was, indeed, a grand thing. However, I couldn't help feeling that if a guy in a strange costume shows up threatening to crash an asteroid into a Day Care Center, you don't stop to consider whether or not the crater could be paved over and used for extra parking spaces. You wade in, fists flying, and beat the guy into a bloody pulp.

"On the other hand, it'll take some time for the newly

infected crops to mature. While we're all waiting, millions of people would die of starvation. Even if we already had a stockpile of the new foods, we'd still have problems with distribution. Some experts believe that we already have enough food to feed everyone, we just can't get it to where it's needed most.

He popped a panel off the side of his contraption and peered at the thing's innards with a dubious expression while he continued talking.

"In some of these Third World countries, you can't get past the government corruption to help the people who need it. Then of course, you've got the problem of spoilage, vermin, black market sales. There are a lot of factors to consider. I can't believe Thanatos is completely oblivious to all of that."

"Oh." Maybe Trav was making some sense after all.

"Oh, indeed. Besides, for a guy who took so much trouble with his outfit, his great big evil plan doesn't have a heck of a lot of flash to it, ya know? He's not showing off, or complicating things to prove how much smarter than everyone else he is."

"Do you mean like Erica and that whirlpool thing she did?" My lungs still ached over that one. I must have inhaled half the harbor before I finally stopped her.

"Yeah. The more I think about it, the more it seems to me that his demand is ridiculously low. What the hell?" He interrupted himself and stuck his hand into the open panel. There was a spark and he yelped, whipping his hand back and plunging a finger into his mouth. "Ouch," he said sheepishly.

"How do you think I felt?" I muttered.

He snatched a wrench from his workbench, thrust it haphazardly into the machine's innards and sort of whooshed it around.

"Let's look at it from a different angle. What if he doesn't think of himself as a bad guy at all? What if we're seeing some kind of warped altruism? Maybe the money's just a pretense. What if what Thanatos *really* wants is exactly the same thing Jackson and Peter want?"

"It's still a terrorist threat, isn't it?"

"Well, yeah. I suppose it is. But he may think that his motives are pure. If so, can you think of a better way of forcing the whole world to accept a new food source? Just spread the shit around and infect everything you can. Don't give anybody a choice."

"Are you sure you want to be doing that?"

"Doing what?"

"That motion with the wrench. Isn't there a lot of delicate stuff in there? Not that I don't have *complete* confidence in you, but since *I'm* the one bound to the table underneath it, and *you're* the one battering the hell out of that thing's insides with a heavy metal tool…"

"Honestly, Alec, you can be such an old lady sometimes." He slid the panel closed. "But if that's his game, why ask for ransom at all?"

He was only half concentrating on talking to me. Unfortunately, that meant he was also only half concentrating on twisting dials and flipping switches, which I found very worrisome when the ominous crackling humming sound started up again.

I shrugged as best as I could, given that I was still strapped down.

"A whim? Maybe he wants to re-decorate his lair and has expensive taste in furniture? Maybe he wants to start a designer line of skin-tight black leather casual wear? Maybe he needs to recoup a bad investment in artificial earthquake generating technology? Who knows? Evil always thinks it has a good reason for doing what it does."

"So that's why Captain Dirigible robs all those banks?" Travis said, sarcastically, while he continued to tinker. "He donates it all to charity."

"I'm not talking about greed. I'm talking about thinking that the end justifies the means. Just like you said. Look at the Caterpillar, fr'instance. He wants to protect a bunch of endangered species. Wiping out the human population of half a continent is just collateral damage as far as he's concerned."

Travis mulled it over. I was grateful for the delay. The machine was emitting that pulsing sound again and the tip was already glowing. A moment later, he shook his head violently.

"I don't buy it. There's something weird about the cash. The amount isn't just low, it's too specific. I'm thinking he *needs* it for something. Heck, you can't even take in a halfway decent heist movie nowadays where the bad guys don't get away with half a billion in loot. We've got to be missing something. So long as this food virus works, there has to be another reason why he's not making demands as outrageous as…well…as outrageous as that ridiculous cape he was twirling."

"You noticed that, too, huh?" I couldn't keep the longing from my voice. "It's much more impressive than mine."

"Don't even think about it. You may be strong, Alec. But you are not the most graceful person on the planet. I can just see you getting that damned thing tangled around your legs at the wrong time and…"

"Yeah, yeah," I agreed grumpily. "But a girl can dream, can't she?"

He grunted. "Dream all you want. You ready?"

"Thanks for asking this time," I muttered.

My eyes widened when I caught a glimpse of the sheet of cloth draped over a chair.

"Travis! Wait!"

"Chill, Alec. It's still powering up."

"But…"

"In any case," he barreled right over me, "if you and I have learned anything from experience, it's that no matter how much we think we know what the bad guys are gonna do, they end up doing something completely unexpected."

"That's true," I agreed quickly and nervously. "Er, didn't you forget something?"

"Forget something?" He paused for an instant. "I don't think so."

"The sheet! You forgot to cover me with the sheet!"

I barely managed to keep the panic from my voice. No matter how much I might have griped about the thin cover being a piece of crap, I was fully aware that whatever properties it possessed were the only things that had mitigated the effects of the Hot Hammer Gun. I was also abundantly conscious of the fact that, without it, nothing stood between my naked chest and a fair amount of pain.

"I have no idea what Thanatos has in store for tomorrow,

but it's not gonna be pretty. I think the Whirlwind needs to make an appearance. Besides..." He switched subjects adroitly. "We're not using the fabric this time, Alec. I *told* you I need to get baselines."

I glanced at the screen and saw that all the bars were well into the red again. The mechanism engaged with another *crack!* This time, it felt like a white-hot bulldozer slammed into my chest. Just before I passed out, I had time for one brief thought:

When I regained consciousness, if I caught Travis swinging another canister at my middle, I had some very definite ideas about where I was going to put it when I gave it back to him.

CHAPTER TEN

For an altruist like Jackson Greene, hatred was a tough emotion to muster. He was no stranger to anger, and he had long since gotten annoyance and irritation down pat. But true hatred had always been beyond him. Even in the face of some pretty despicable behavior–and Jackson had certainly seen his share of that–his instincts were to put aside enmity in favor of a better understanding about the causes that drive men to do terrible things to their fellows.

The oxygen mask, however, was a fair target.

Jackson hated it more than he'd thought it was possible for him to hate anything. True, it helped him to continue breathing while his lungs were failing. But Jackson had vital information for Peter and the mask made it impossible to communicate. Each time he struggled to remove it, Peter replaced it with a mild rebuke. Though he appreciated the boy's concern for his well-being, it was driving Jackson Greene crazy.

Again, he tried to claw the mask from his face. Again, Peter stopped him.

"For heaven's sake, Jackson, cut it out." Peter smiled, frustrated but affectionate. "There's nothing you have to tell me about Greene Genes that I don't already know. You need to relax and conserve your strength."

Unfortunately, there was still something about Feed the World, that Peter did *not* know, and Jackson desperately needed to tell him. How could he get rid of the damned mask? Inspired, he motioned toward the pitcher on the side table.

"Water?"

Jackson nodded. Peter poured a small amount into the

plastic cup and plopped a straw into it. Holding the cup in one hand, Peter *finally* removed the damned mask so Jackson could drink.

"Feed the World..." the old man whispered.

"I know." Peter shushed him. "I promise we'll get it back on track. Don't worry..."

"No," he gasped. "Copy!"

Peter blinked a few times and froze with the cup of water halfway to Jackson's mouth.

"What?"

"C...copy." The old man motioned for the water and, once he'd moistened his tongue he drew in a ragged breath for speech. "Bradley's house. In his safe."

"He kept a copy?" Peter was stunned. "Sweet Jesus, Jackson! Why didn't you say something before?"

Greene grimaced weakly. "Wasn't thinking. The explosion... shock. Then, the drugs. Mind fuzzy. Not at my best." He grunted and cleared his throat. "Knew there was something but...forgot what."

"The combination?" Peter leaned forward eagerly.

"Bio..." His frail body was wracked with coughing before he could continue. "Bio-locked. DNA reader."

He could see young Peter's mind racing. Silently, he urged him understand how he might go about saving the project.

"There's *tons* of DNA we could use! His comb, tooth brushes..."

Jackson nodded encouragement.

"We have people to code it properly, put it in the proper format..."

Jackson frowned and hoped he could communicate what he had to say. "Three-Two-Three issues." Another coughing spasm. "Maybe Brad really solved them?"

"If that's true...do you know what this could mean? Oh..." He blushed and looked foolish. "Of course you do."

Peter saw him struggling to breathe and replaced the oxygen mask.

"I have to get whatever's in that safe right away."

"Go," Jackson mouthed through the plastic shield. He

doubted Peter heard him but his intent was abundantly clear.

"I'll be back," the younger man called as he raced out the door.

Exhausted from the effort, Jackson slumped against the pillows. It was up to Peter now. Knowing that there was nothing more he could do was strangely relaxing, and he drifted into sleep. When he awoke several hours later, he found that night had fallen and his pain had worsened. He needed more medication but he couldn't find the contraption to summon the nurse.

His search for the call mechanism halted abruptly. An ominous figure stood quietly in the corner of the room. The intruder sensed that he was awake and stepped forward. The black cape rustled as it slid across the floor. Jackson knew immediately who it was.

"Did you really think," the mechanically-altered voice whispered, "that I wouldn't keep an eye on you?"

"No!" The word didn't need to be fully voiced to reflect his horror.

"I'm sorry for this," Thanatos said. "But your life is about to end anyway. There are more important things at stake."

Gently, Thanatos removed the oxygen mask and pulled the pillow from underneath the old man's shoulders, leaving him flat on his back. The new position made breathing even more difficult.

"I would have preferred to let Nature take her course. Unfortunately, I can't risk the delay."

The pillow hovered, poised above Jackson's face. Panic gave him the strength to summon enough breath for one last cry.

"Peter!"

The pillow came down.

"I don't think Peter Camry will be much of a problem any more, do you?" Thanatos asked.

Moments later, Jackson Greene's feeble struggles had halted. The hated mask was back in place and the oxygen continued to flow.

It did him little good.

CHAPTER ELEVEN

Back when Old Man Lacey was alive, the Farmers Market was the most popular family weekend destination in all of Centerport County. After he passed, his daughters were neither farmers nor businesswomen and, when they couldn't sustain the business, the property was seized for unpaid taxes. Eventually, Greene Genes leased it, converted it into a testing facility, and erected a twelve-foot high fence around the whole place to keep out the curious. Now, the farm was off-limits to all but authorized personnel. It was here that the trial run of the new pesticide was to take place and, if Thanatos' threat was legit, the Whirlwind needed to be on hand.

Between the scientists intent on whatever they were intent upon, and the veritable battalion of cops on hand to protect them, the area was an anthill of frenetic activity. I made a pit stop to check in with Gretchen and make sure she knew I'd arrived.

"Keep an eye out," she said brusquely when she saw me.

"Gee, thanks Gretch. How about, 'Great to see you! See any good movies lately? Did you ever manage to clear up that rash?'"

She responded with a scowl while she barked commands to her underlings into her walkie talkie.

"I guess I'll just mosey up to the top of that big old barn to get a better view of the festivities, eh?"

"Water tower's better," she noted, and dismissed me by turning her attention back to the walkie-talkie.

I came very close to saying something about being taken for granted but, given the fervor with which she was growling commands, I figured that it was probably best not to provoke her. Instead, I hauled my tightly muscled little butt across the barnyard and up the rusty ladder to the top of the tower. Once there, I paused for a moment to strike a pose with my cape dramatically billowing behind me, and my chest inflated heroically, just in case any of the paparazzi happened to be in the area looking for a photo op.

Standing that way was not only uncomfortable but, since it meant I was fully exposed to attacks from death rays and bazookas, it was also silly. I soon abandoned it and dropped into a crouch before closing my eyes and extending my senses. If Thanatos was on the scene already, it would be a good idea for me to know about it. Unfortunately, all the busy bees rushing hither and yon were distorting any signals I could pick up. Given the interference, I'd be lucky to sense a bad guy at all before he snuck up behind me and yelled, "Boo!

It took less than an hour for the Greene Genes people to get ready, but it seemed like I was perched up there for days. Finally, the hustle and bustle faded and everyone took their assigned positions. I knew that if something was going to happen, it would happen soon. I felt a sense of foreboding and, instinctively, I scanned the ground three stories below to see if I could locate Peter just in case. No matter how many civilians might be threatened by whatever Thanatos had in mind, my first priority was damned well going to be protecting my husband. But I couldn't spot him. Hopefully, he was tucked out of harm's way, running things from the safety of one of the big SUVs with the huge dish antennas that were parked some distance from the barnyard.

I'm a city boy at heart. Nevertheless, I've watched enough *Green Acres* reruns, not to mention that cinema classic, *Lassoed Young Cowboy Studs*, to be able to identify basic farm equipment. You know, tractors, pickup trucks, windmills, cows...that sort of thing. The contraption that trundled out of Lacey's barn was nothing like any farm equipment I'd ever seen. The top half looked like an antique fire truck, with nozzles and hoses pointing in all directions. The bottom part had treads like a tank. Adding to the impression that Ah-nald was about to burst from the hatch, bare-chested except for some sweat and bandoliers, the driver's cab was heavily armored. It reminded me of a mobile version of one of those bunkers you see in 1950s sci-fi movies where all the generals hang out to watch the nuclear testing.

It putt-putted toward a small plot of corn that was insulated from the rest of the fields by a tenting of clear plastic sheeting hung on a metal frame. A bunch of people in bio hazard suits let it into the makeshift dome and then made quite a production number out of making sure the plastic was securely sealed behind it. A warning bell sounded and, simultaneously, a white fluid erupted from all of the nozzles, thick enough to coat the plastic and completely obscure anyone's ability to see inside. It continued for quite a while, certainly long enough for me to have drained the hot water heater should I have taken that long of a shower at home. Eventually, the bell rang a second time, and the hoses ceased their hissing.

There was a little square area attached to one side of the dome, also covered in plastic, sort of like an airlock on a space ship. As it turned out, that was pretty much what it was. Someone in a hazmat suit, presumably the driver of the tank-like thing, exited the main part of the dome and stepped into it. Immediately, pressure hoses kicked in from all sides with enough force to knock him to his knees. He hunkered down under the onslaught and was engulfed in a small mountain of disinfectant foam. Impressed, I made a mental note to ask Peter if we could borrow the hoses and give the cars a good wash. Eventually, the spray subsided to a trickle and the man was whisked into a nearby van with a red medical cross on the side.

The test *seemed* to have gone off without a hitch. If Thanatos intended to pull anything, it would have to be soon. As a precaution, I extended my senses again but, even before I picked anything up, I heard the whirring sound of something mechanical quickly coming up behind me. I spun around fast enough for my cape to twirl. I stopped, stunned.

I felt no fear. I wasn't the slightest bit intimidated. What I was, was envious. Though the jury was still out on whether Thanatos was insane, or clever, no one could deny that the guy had a marvelous sense of theater and knew how to make an entrance.

In person, his body was even more impressive than it looked

in the video. Next to Thanatos's get-up, George Clooney's and Chris O'Donnell's bat suits were barely a step above burlap sacks. And that cape! I lusted for the cape almost as desperately as I lusted to see Thanatos without the cape.

The hell with the cape. If truth be told, I lusted to see Thanatos without *anything* between him and the brightly shining sun but a thin film of baby oil.

And then I spotted the boots.

The boots were a foot fetishist's wet dream come true. I've never been into feet. Nor am I one of those gay men who has three hundred pairs of shoes in his closet. I've got sneakers for the gym, my day-to-day office shoes, an old pair of work shoes that I wear when I'm doing stuff around the house, and a pair of Cole Haan's that I wear with a suit whenever Peter and I go to a nice place for dinner. Yet, if I'd seen Thanatos' boots on sale at the mall, I'd have been sorely tempted. Not only did they extend almost to his knees, they managed to highlight that muscled bump in his calves that no amount of squats will get you unless you're genetically predisposed to it. Sable black, the supple leather was so highly polished that it looked like it had been painted onto him and was still wet.

The pièce de résistance, though, was the scooter. Actually, it was more like a flying surfboard than a scooter, but it had a steering column at the front, and wing-like embellishments extended from both sides to create a batwing effect. Naturally, it was painted as black as molten tar. I gave Thanatos points for consistency even if his color scheme was a bit predictable.

It was decorated with a lot of gears and pistons which, for all I knew, might have actually served some real purpose. In a lot of ways, the design reminded me of Captain Dirigible's penchant for Steam Punk except that Thanatos' taste seemed to be more Gothically inspired. Fixed between the handlebars like a ship's masthead, there was a sculpted mask that was the twin to the one Thanatos' was wearing.

"A little warm for leather, isn't it?" I called out.

"Glass houses," he said. "Spandex doesn't breathe particularly well either. And what *is* it with you and that color?" He shook his head with mock sadness at my lack of taste. "Found a parking space for your unicorn, did you?"

I bristled and mimed rolling up my sleeves. "I really do hope those muscles aren't just for show. It'll make it that much more challenging to beat you to a pulp before I haul you in."

There was a long pause during which he seemed to be waiting.

"That's it?" he finally asked. "I'd expected something snappier from the Whirlwind."

I felt warmth rising into my cheeks when I realized that he was actually *amused* by me!

"Will snapping closed the handcuffs be snappy enough for you?"

"Oh dear." His lips curled downwards in what I thought was a frown. Under the mask, it was hard to tell. "I was really looking forward to experiencing some of that infamous Whirlwind wit first hand. Now you've gone and ruined my illusions." He made that tongue-clucking *tsk* sound that always sounds sarcastic... usually because it *is* sarcastic. "Whatever can we do to restore my faith in you?"

I was annoyed, mostly because the smug prick was right. Usually, I'm far smoother and more urbane. There was something about him—aside from all those muscles staring me in the face—that was throwing me off. It sure as heck wasn't his voice. The artificial distortion device that he was using made him sound like a kitchen dispose-all. The gizmo he was using was mounted on a little leather collar...

...pressed against the base of the sinewed column of his throat...

...just above the deep indentation between his pectorals...

...right at the place where his chest flared into twin muscled slabs of...

I shook my head to clear it.

"You're one to talk. A *nipple* suit?" I scoffed.

Damn, I couldn't shift my focus from the guy's spectacular chest!

"Nipples have their uses," he crooned.

Something about the way he said it made my knees go all watery. I was a married man, dammit! And yet...

He fiddled with a switch and put his devil-mobile into Park, before he stepped effortlessly onto the surface of the water tower. Thanatos moved like a panther, gracefully, with a kind of power lurking beneath the surface, but not hidden so deeply that it doesn't let you know how powerful it is. Now that he was only a few yards away, I could see that I'd been wrong about him wearing body armor. The physique he displayed so shamelessly beneath its sheaf of supple leather was genuine. For long seconds, I stood there, drinking in every inch of him and doing my best not to drool. Under different circumstances, the tightness at my groin might have been quite pleasant.

Fortunately, I remembered in time that Thanatos was a fiend who had threatened hundreds of people's lives. To keep my briefs from getting any tighter, I tore my gaze away from his torso and focused on his face.

In retrospect, that may not have been the best idea I'd ever had.

I've always been a sucker for guys with sexy eyes. Peter, for example, has really unusual, dark green eyes. I never tire of looking into them–especially when we're both naked and breathing really hard. To my surprise, Thanatos' eyes had a similar effect on me.

Their color was hard to judge. The cowl left bare a small area around each eye, and he'd covered the exposed flesh with make-up that had a weird reflective quality. Because of it, the best I could say was that his eyes were...well...not brown. I leaned forward, entranced, trying to get a better look. They were too dark to be blue, but they didn't seem green either. Just when I was sure they were hazel, he inclined his head a tiny bit so that his irises caught the light and looked gray. In any case, the way they were stimulating my libido had little to do with their exact color.

The two of us stood there for several minutes, as if caught in some kind of stalemate, until I managed to get both my breathing and my hormones under control.

"You're cute." When he finally broke the silence, he sounded surprised.

One hand reached out as if to take my chin. I stepped back. As aroused as I was, I'm not stupid.

"Under that mask," he continued, "there is some definite cuteness going on. I usually prefer blonds but, in your case, I'd be tempted to make an exception. It's a pity we didn't meet under less adversarial circumstances."

Okay Alec, I thought. *Pull yourself together and get down to business.*

"I'm told," I shot back, "there are some very cute guys in the Centerport Penitentiary. Of course, they don't bathe regularly and they like to be called Crusher or Big Daddy. Maybe you could tell me what's it like sharing a shower with thirty gang-bangers who confuse spit with KY. Oh, wait!" I smacked my forehead with one palm. "I forgot. You haven't met them. Yet."

It was my turn to be surprised when Thanatos burst out laughing.

"Now, *that* is the Whirlwind I've heard so much about."

"I suppose..." I wanted to keep the guy talking, *anything* to take my mind off that damned body of his that was making me crazy. "I suppose you have no intention of coming along quietly? You should think about it. So far, you're only looking at extortion."

"You're wrong about that, Cuteness. Don't forget arson, kidnaping, and a murder or two, though that last couldn't be avoided. I'm afraid that means I won't be coming along quietly. I won't be coming along at all. In fact, the main reason I showed up today was to meet the Whirlwind."

"I'm flattered." I kept all emotion out of my voice, but it was rough. He'd called me cute. I'd have preferred being called hot or studly, but cute would do just fine. Especially since he'd said it *three* times!

"You should be. I confess there's an ulterior motive as well. I need to be certain that you understand me."

"Understand you?"

He nodded.

"That I am capable of doing exactly what I threatened to do."

The attraction dimmed and the chemistry between us–and I was positive it was mutual–soured.

"Roughly twelve hours from now, give or take, some of the

ground crew down there will begin to experience distress." He waved one gloved hand to take in the scientists and cops below.

"Feed the World. You activated the Three-Two-Three variant."

"I'm impressed. Did you figure that out all by yourself?"

I felt a spasm of what was probably a sympathetic pain in the center of my chest while I struggled to remember the details of what Travis had told me. Understandably, my attention had been elsewhere at the time.

"Except that there is no tainted produce," I said, maybe a little too smugly. "You haven't had time to grow any. Snow White can't eat the poisoned apple if it doesn't exist yet. As far as I'm concerned, it's all blah, blah, blah at this point."

"Suddenly...not so impressed."

He sounded disappointed and, in spite of myself, I felt like I'd let him down.

"You may want to have someone take a look at this."

He tossed a small, black plastic cube at me but it fell short. I had to move my foot to keep it from sliding down the curve of the water tower.

"Don't presume that this is the actual technology." He wagged a finger. "Wouldn't want to give you a chance to reverse engineer things too quickly. But it should provide enough evidence that I am capable of following through."

He spun around, incidentally giving me my first glimpse of his equally incredible butt, and took a step toward the demonic flying skateboard.

"Where the hell do you think you're going? You're under arrest."

"Please..." He drew the word out. "Let's not be tiresome, shall we? Who's going to stop me? You?"

"Damned straight," I muttered.

"Not from what I can tell."

A click sounded when he locked one boot onto the stirrup that kept him from falling off the scooter. I expected him to rev the engine like a demonic biker in some hellish motorcycle gang and peel off into the sky. But he paused before fixing the second boot into place. He stood there, a midnight specter astride his scooter, so still that it bordered on being spooky.

I got a clear impression that there was something troubling him. It wasn't compassion, and it sure as heck wasn't any doubt about doing what he had threatened to do. But I sensed a hesitation nonetheless. The silence lengthened for a good minute or so.

"Stand aside, my friend."

All the flippancy was gone; there was no more sarcasm. It was a command, but it was uttered softly and with a quiet intensity.

"I'm prepared to take whatever steps necessary to get what I want." His next words, unless I was mistaken, held some very sincere regret. "I didn't realize you'd be so attractive. You have a very sweet quality that doesn't quite translate in your TV interviews. No offense, but you tend come across as a little..." He tapped his temple. "...Dim."

Before I could think of a clever riposte, he went on.

"In person though..."

Other than my husband, the last person who'd looked at me with that much naked lust was Erica the Eel. When she did it, it was creepy as hell. Somehow, I didn't much mind when it came from Thanatos.

"I don't want to hurt you," he said. "Or kill you. But that's exactly what will happen if you persist in interfering. Please, for your own sake and the sake of anyone who loves you, stand aside."

"Can't do that." My muscles tensed. I prepared myself to take him down.

"Pity."

I launched myself at him. Unfortunately, as I believe I've mentioned before, I am *not* the most graceful person in the world.

I caught him around the waist just as he placed his second foot onto the scooter. What I hadn't counted on was the vehicle's inability to support both our weights. It slid down the slope of the tower and keeled over. The next thing I knew, the scooter was hovering upside down in midair; Thanatos was hanging from the scooter by one foot.

And I was hanging from Thanatos.

"Idiot!"

The flirtatious tone was gone. He snarled the word. He grabbed my forearms, and tried to pry my grip loose from around his middle.

I wasn't having any of it. I shifted position and started climbing up his body which, given that he was upside down, was more like climbing *down* his body, toward his feet. He wriggled to get free but I managed to hang on, uncomfortably aware of how close my face was to his groin, and vice versa. Thanatos grunted and jackknifed so he could reach the scooter's controls. He flipped a switch and the engine took on a high-pitched whine. The contraption rose a few feet.

"Get...off!"

The guy packed a really good punch. My solar plexus can testify to it.

"Not so fast."

Hand over hand, I clawed up his thighs and onto his calves. If I could just reach the edge of the scooter, I could haul myself on top of...well, on top of the bottom. But Thanatos' costume was slippery. I lost my grip and slid back a little. I glanced down, worried about how far above the ground we were and how much the fall would hurt. As a last resort, I could probably figure a way to knock the both of us out of the sky. I knew that at least one of us would survive the fall. As for Thanatos...would I be the only one who was upset because an arch villain was squashed like road kill?

I pushed aside my regrets, in advance, and readied myself to make my move. I was trying to judge the distance when...

"Holy shit!"

It wasn't the pain, because it didn't actually hurt. Mostly, I felt pressure. It was the mental image of what was happening that was so off-putting. The bastard was *biting* into my *crotch*!

"Are you nuts?"

I let go with one hand to make a fist and deliver a mighty wallop to return the favor.

My punch had more of an impact than his bite. He grunted in pain and, I suspect, involuntarily did something to the scooter's controls. The warp drive or whatever kicked in, and the water tower receded behind us as we soared skyward. As we ascended, I found my attraction to full length capes waning; his was tangled around my feet, effectively preventing me from kicking free.

"You fool!"

I'd certainly heard *that* before, and from far more experienced arch villains than Thanatos was.

Upward we flew, ever upward until we were several hundred feet above the water tower. Over the whining of the scooter, I imagined I could hear shocked gasps from the onlookers below. I most *definitely* heard shouts of alarm when the engine abruptly overloaded, belched smoke, and cut out completely.

I had just enough time to utter the *Oh!* part of *Oh, shit!*

We plummeted like a trio of bricks until all three of us–Thanatos, the devil-mobile, and me–smashed into the water tower. I'd been expecting the bone-crushing crunch of my body impacting with the asphalt parking lot or, at least, that some of my organs would be jellied when I plowed an extremely deep furrow in one of the fields. So, the chilly water closing over my head surprised the hell out of me. The unexpected dousing, the shock of cold, and the several gallons of water I swallowed when I opened my mouth to curse a blue streak, all conspired to make me lose my grip.

I broke the surface, sputtering and coughing. Aside from a shaft of sunlight bleeding through the hole above me, the inside of the tower was murky and dark. I treaded water and thrashed wildly as I spun myself around and foolishly tried to see into all the corners of a round space. All I needed was for Thanatos to jump me from behind–and *not* in a good way! When I wasn't instantly set upon, my thoughts calmed and I realized that, unless he'd come loose in the crash, there was a good chance that Thanatos' foot was still locked onto the scooter. The weight of the thing would have dragged him straight to the bottom. Not unaware of the irony of the Whirlwind needing to rescue a bad guy, no matter how hunky, I took a deep breath, preparing to submerge and look for him.

I needn't have bothered.

Apparently, the scooter's engine didn't like being wet any more than I did.

The force of the explosion momentarily pinned me against the roof of the tower. All around me, the water bubbled and sloshed madly. I had time to grab a single gulp of air before my body was seized by a powerful suction from below. As I was drawn through the churning maelstrom, I glimpsed a large rupture in the bottom of the tank and I realized that I was being sucked straight for it. I was moving too fast to grab the broken boards at the edge and stop myself from hurtling through. Rather than risking the attempt and tearing off a limb, I extended both arms above my head, formed my hands into fists, and straightened my spine. With any luck, I'd emerge from the tank with the grace of a professional high diver, and not with my arms and legs flailing helplessly.

The bad news is that I wasn't entirely successful. The good news is that there was no one waiting inside the barn with a cell phone to record my shame.

I shot out of the tank at an angle, moving like a rocket. Happily, soaring through the air like that is not a very relaxing experience, so my body remained tensed. More importantly, some instinct told me to keep my fists clenched in front of me like a human pile-driver. It was the only thing that kept me from hitting the barn face-first.

Smashing through the wood siding hurt. Smashing through the thick wooden beams hurt even more. Smashing into the side of the abandoned tractor hurt the most. But that was just my experience. If you ever succumb to a masochistic urge to throw yourself through barn siding, support beams, and rusty farm equipment–in that order–your opinion may differ.

At least, thanks to Travis' genius, the costume remained intact when it hit all those metal blades. Nudity, even partial nudity, would only have added to my hurt and shame. As it was, I felt like I'd just been forced through a mechanical thresher which, come to think of it, is a fairly accurate description of what happened.

Shortly after I landed, the huge double doors swung open. Gretchen and a small army of police burst into the barn.

"My God! Are you all right? Whirlwind?"

"Ouch." I muttered.

Given a few minutes to make sure that my intestines were still inside my body *and* attached at both ends, I could probably have some up with some witty line of deathless prose. But everything *hurt*, so I took the easy way out.

"Ouch," I repeated louder.

A half dozen eager pairs of hands helped me wobble to my feet. I had a few bad moments while I waited for my vision to clear because it looked to me like Gretchen was having an epileptic fit or was being attacked by killer bees. Then, it dawned on me that her spastic mime was her way of letting me know that some ancient wisps of hay were clinging to my hair and shoulders, and making me look like a turquoise Phyllis Diller. Nodding silent thanks–a mistake because it started my head spinning again–I brushed away as much of the chaff as I could.

"Where's Thanatos?"

I'd like to see *anyone* go through what I had just gone through and not sound like Mickey Mouse. I cleared my throat and tried again.

"Did you nab the sonofabitch?"

I stumbled out of the barn with Gretchen at my side, and with the rest of the cops in our wake. We emerged just in time to see a trail of black smoke vanishing in the direction of Centerport.

"How...?" I couldn't figure out how he'd gotten away. "I thought the Devil Scooter blew up."

"The Devil Scooter?"

"That thing he was riding. The skateboard with the...demon thing where the mermaid goes."

"Are you sure you don't need to see a doctor?" she asked.

I shook my head, which I discovered gave me the same headache as nodding did.

"Whatever it was, he's gone now," she said.

"Dammit."

"But he left a little gift behind." She grinned and held up the little black tube. "It fell off the roof while you two were trading recipes and one of my guys snagged it before it hit the ground."

"You might not want to look quite so happy about it. It's not some clue you tripped over. He wanted me to have it. I'm pretty sure that we're not gonna be thrilled by what's inside."

My brain eventually stopped slamming itself against the inside of my skull, and I gazed after the fading wisps of the smoke trail with regret. I was disappointed, of course, that Thanatos had given us the slip. I was even more disappointed that I didn't get a chance for a last look at his magnificent butt while he made his escape.

I tried to focus on Peter. On how much we loved each other. On how the sex between us was always fantastic and often mind-boggling. But thoughts of the way Thanatos' muscles moved under his ebony costume kept distracting me.

What *was* it about this guy that stirred me up so?

And what the hell was I gonna do about it?

CHAPTER TWELVE

"He's going to spread the virus by air, isn't he?"

Gretchen sat at our kitchen counter in an almost tangible cloud of gloom. She looked as sad as a cocker spaniel pup whose favorite squeaky toy has been taken away to be washed. The poor doggy doesn't understand that he'll get it back. Gretchen was a lot like that spaniel except, since her blouse was stained and mis-buttoned, and she'd worn several holes in her slacks, I'd say the better analogy would be to a junkyard mutt.

"Not quite. But he's going to try," Travis told her. "Sweet Jesus, Alec! This mayo's so old even I'm tempted not to eat it. When did you decide to open up the Ptomaine Palace?"

The first part of Travis's statement was muffled, mostly because his head and shoulders were engulfed in my refrigerator while he rummaged for more calories to pack onto his waist.

"That's the egg mayo. We must have forgotten to throw it out when we switched to the soy-based stuff. Besides, fruit's healthier for you."

I plucked an orange from the bowl we kept on the counter and held it up so that he could see what an actual piece of healthy food looked like.

Travis acknowledged the fruit with the barest of grunts, and turned his back on it. He unscrewed the top of the mayonnaise jar and spooned a huge dollop of the stuff onto a slice of raisin toast. It may have been due to some strange effect of the overhead light, but I'm pretty sure that mayonnaise isn't supposed to be quite that shade of bright yellow. My revulsion must have shown on my face.

"Don't worry." He licked the spoon with gusto and I shuddered. "Cast iron gut. Galvanized rubber. Stainless steel. You should be more careful, kiddo. Peter doesn't have the Whirlwind's constitution."

"Oh, I've known Whirlwind to suffer a Morning After or two," Gretchen couldn't resist pointing out.

"I'm so grateful that I can always count on you being there to rub my face in it," I assured her with acid sweetness.

"Speaking of rubbing your face...what the hell were you guys *doing* up there in midair? From the ground–and from the photo on the front page of the Centerport Chronicle–it looked like you two were getting hot and heavy."

"Nanoprobes," Travis said.

"No," Gretchen said. "I'm pretty sure it was sixty-nine."

"Technically, it's not airborne. Not on its own. I think he's planning on using nanoprobes. I'll explain if you two kids will stop bickering for a minute."

"I'm a full-grown woman, Travis, not a kid."

"That you are, Gretchen, my heart. That you are."

She blushed and quickly tried to change the subject. "Is it okay to talk about this when Peter could be home any minute?"

"About what? About you and Travis having a romantic candlelight dinner somewhere?"

Her flush deepened.

"He's holed up with the Greene Genes lawyers," I told them, "and won't be home until late. Seems the company could get sued for this even though it's all because of Thanatos."

She nodded. Evidently, she understood the machinations of the legal system better than I did.

"What's this business about nanoprobes?"

Travis chewed lustily for a moment; a little mayo clung to one corner of his mouth. He spied a liter bottle of soda and used it to wash everything down. He drank directly from the bottle, which always grosses me out.

"Ugh. Diet." He grimaced at the label.

"Which you could use," I pointed out.

"That's what was in the black tube he left behind. Nanoprobes. Inert ones, but they still make his point. The fact that he even has them suggests that he's quite capable of carrying out his threat. I'm beginning to suspect that was part of Brad Harmon's focus before he was killed. He was trying to adapt nanoprobes to solve his Three-Two-Three problem."

"What are nanoprobes?" I asked.

"That's a more complicated question than you'd suppose," he said. "You could think of them like microscopic robots."

"Like that old movie with Raquel Welch?" I asked. "Where they take the miniature submarine into the guy's body and almost get eaten up by the critters in his blood?"

Travis chuckled. "Sort of. Except they're not mechanical. We don't build them. We grow them from living cells and 'program' them for a specific task."

"Like what?"

"Let's say you've got a patient with inoperable brain cancer. You program special nanoprobes to target and attack the cancerous cells. In a single syringe, you could inject a few hundred thousand of them into your patient. Then, you let them multiply into a brain cancer eating army. It's not *quite* that simple, of course. You'd have to worry about the body's immune system counter-attacking, for example. But that's the theory at least."

While he was talking, he used the handle of the dirty mayo spoon to scoop a huge glob of peanut butter out of a different jar and spread in onto his toast. He topped that with a couple of sliced pickles and some leftover cottage cheese.

"I think that Thanatos has developed a way to use nanoprobes to transmit the toxic variant of the Feed the World virus directly from host to host. That is, people wouldn't have to eat the tainted food in order to be affected."

He doused the sandwich filling with hot sauce and covered the mess with another slice of cinnamon toast. I felt my gorge rise.

"Could *you* reverse engineer it?' Gretch wanted to know. "Develop a vaccine maybe?"

Travis shook his head and her expression fell even further.

"We'll have to leave that to the folks at Greene Genes. I may be brilliant but..." He waited for compliments that never came. "...I'm pretty much a glorified engineer. I've got a good foundation in basic chemistry. But once you bring biology into the mix, not so much."

"This is not making me feel any better," she said.

"Let's assume," Travis went on, "that Brad Harmon already did the bulk of the work. He grew the nanoprobes and tailored them to carry the Feed the World virus. If that's what happened, Thanatos' job was easy. All he had to do was reprogram them. That would require some specialized equipment but as long as he was using preexisting research as a guide, and not just stumbling around blindly, he wouldn't even need an advanced degree to understand how to do it. It's basic lab tech stuff. And that's exactly what was in the vial he left behind."

"Good god." Gretchen blanched.

"Don't get your panties in a twist just yet," Travis reassured her. "Thanatos is a lot different from the bad guys we're used to seeing around here. He's not asking for much, remember?"

"Define 'much'."

He ignored her.

"We should thank our lucky stars that it wasn't someone like the Caterpillar who got his hands on this stuff." He shuddered. "We'd be talking about wiping out humanity as a species. No, I'm even more certain of it now. This guy is strictly about the cash. And *that*, my little bon-bons, tells us something about him that should make us feel a lot better about this situation."

"Oh yeah? What?" Her natural belligerence momentarily eclipsed her despondence.

"Think it through, Gretch. With this kind of technology in his pocket, he could easily get ten times what he asked for. Greed, then, is obviously not his motive. I was right in thinking that this guy needs the money for something specific. That means he's probably not crazy."

"That's one point for our team," I said.

"If I'm right, and he's not one of the usual psychos, I'll bet that he's been very careful to make sure that, even if he releases the virus, it doesn't get out of control."

"He's still threatening mass murder," Gretchen said, irritated. "He's hardly Mary Poppins."

"While he may not object to a few deaths as, well, collateral damage, I don't think his primary goal is killing people."

"The stuff in that little vial would suggest otherwise."

"That's the interesting part," Travis told her.

"What is?"

Gretchen was literally sitting on the edge of her chair to demand the information from him. But Travis was in no rush to alleviate the suspense. Instead of telling her, he took another huge bite out of his disgusting sandwich. I grabbed a paper towel and cleaned up the mélange of mayo, peanut butter, and pickle juice that he dripped onto the counter.

"The nanoprobes in the sample he gave us are duds," he announced with satisfaction.

"Duds?"

"I don't wanna get too technical so, how can I put this? He's waving an unloaded gun. Think of the virus as being the bullets."

"A bluff?"

He shook his head. "I'm not willing to make that wager. Not yet. I can think of too many reasons for him to do it this way. Good reasons. The biggest one is what you said earlier. He doesn't want to risk us being able to reverse engineer the technology. Not to mention giving us an edge in coming up with an antidote."

"Could we do that?" For the first time, she brightened.

"According to what I saw of Brad's notes...yeah. It's not difficult. It takes time more than anything else. Bradley's problem with this Three Two Three bugaboo he created was never about finding a cure for the victims. The thing he was struggling with was how to make sure they didn't get infected in the first place. Still..."

His voice trailed off as a thought occurred to him. When he didn't continue, Gretchen cleared her throat to remind him that we were still there.

"Oh, sorry. It just occurred to me that Thanatos might be having trouble programming the nanos with the pathogen."

"Didn't you just say that wouldn't be a problem for him?"

Travis shrugged.

"I'm brain storming here, guys. Trying to come up with reasons why the nanos he gave us were empty. The only way to know for sure is for us to get our hands on a sample of the actual organism."

"How the hell are we supposed to do that?" Gretchen looked like she was on the verge of sinking into a funk again.

"We don't," Travis told her. "Alec does."

That seemed to perk her up, I'm sorry to say.

"I see…"

She looked at me in this measuring way that I did not like one bit.

"Whirlwind's biochemistry should be able to resist the results of being infected," Travis continued.

"*Should?*" The squeak was back in my voice.

"Yeah. You may not realize it, Alec, but you catch colds just like normal people. The difference is that you never have the chance to develop any symptoms. Whirlwind's body is just that good at fighting everything off."

I gulped and hoped I misunderstood what he was proposing. "Are you saying…you want me to let these nano-thingies get *inside* me?"

"You're not some kind of alien. You're human. You're just stronger than normal. The thing is, see, that a nanoprobe infection isn't a natural one. It's strong too. I bet they'd be able to survive against your body's natural defenses. At least for a little while. The trick will be getting you into the lab so I can get samples before your immune system kills 'em off. If my theory is correct…"

"*Theory?* You don't *know?*"

Travis shook his head cheerfully.

"There is no way I'm gonna risk being assimilated by pint-sized Borgs."

I turned to Gretchen for support, but she was much happier now that we had a plan, even if it was at my expense.

"We'll have to figure out a way to get you and Thanatos together again. I haven't yet met a bad guy who didn't want a chance to get the Whirlwind out of the way. We only have to present him with the opportunity," she enthused.

"This is *not* the top item on my bucket list, gang." I backed away from the two of them until I hit the kitchen wall and couldn't go any further unless I was willing to re-plaster. "Look, I'm all for plunging into a roaring inferno to rescue some little girl's kitten. If you need someone to face down a battalion of armed psychopaths bare-handed, or to stop a runaway freight train from smashing into a bus full of nuns, I'm your guy. But we're talking about *diseases* here. Serious sickness, the kind that you can't cure with warm blankets and chicken soup."

"Alec..."

"Don't you 'Alec' me!" I retreated behind the counter. "I have no desire to end up like that blueberry girl in *Willie Wonka*."

"Stop being such a baby."

"I have a loving husband. I have a very successful business. I am a pillar of this community. Richie even gave me a plaque that says so. Hell, I was the secretary for the Chamber of Commerce for a couple of months before they saw my handwriting and found out they couldn't read the meeting minutes. That's a lot to risk."

"If Travis says he can do it..."

"That is exactly my point. He did *not* say he can do it. He only thinks he *might* be able to do it."

"I doubt it would be life-threatening for you, Alec. In a worst-case scenario if it turns out that your system can't fight it off, you might have to eat some specially grown food for a while until we figure out how to counteract the effects."

"Where would we get this specially grown food, pray tell?" I demanded.

It was a testament to our friendship, I think, that neither one of them would look me directly in the eyes.

"Ah ha! See what I mean? We're not talking about a couple weeks on Lean Cuisine, are we? It's not like I can stop into the market to pick up a dozen eggs, a carton of milk, and some frozen dinners designed for freaking *mutants*, can I?"

"Fine." Gretchen stood and pretended she was ready to leave. "Don't do it. No sweat off my back. We'll just need to be prepared to let thousands of people die because of this maniac. Not that *you* should feel any guilt about that, Alec. You just sit back and keep leasing out your fancy boys while the *real* professionals handle it. I'm sure you won't lose a wink of sleep over it while you're cuddled up with Peter, all nice and cozy…"

She stopped, her mouth dropped open, and her eyes got very round. Then, she smacked her forehead with her palm as if to jostle herself out of being stupid. With an overdone performance like that, Gretchen would never come close to an Oscar nomination but, nevertheless, she made her point.

"Wait! How silly of me to forget! Peter is only *human*, isn't he? Why, he might be as susceptible to this stuff as everyone else. Isn't that right, Travis?"

Wisely, Travis said nothing.

"While Peter is lying there dying, you can just snuggle up to your award from the Chamber of Commerce. Just forget that we asked for your help. You should worry about yourself. Just go about your business."

"Thanatos is my business," I growled before I realized what I'd done.

Gretchen smirked, pleased with herself.

"Fine! If you want the Whirlwind to catch a bad case of Devil Scooter Flu, I'll run right out and catch it. But…" I rounded the counter and approached her ominously. "You will *never* use Pete to get me to do something this stupid *ever* again, d'you hear me? Never ever!"

She looked so damned smug that I wanted to hit something. But there was nothing in the kitchen that could be pulverized without risking questions from Peter about how it got that way. Frustrated, and even though it was kind of girly, the only thing I could think of to release my anger was to stamp my foot. So, I did.

Gretchen made a pouty-face and stamped back. It pissed me off even more, so I stamped again. Travis stamped *his* foot and then Gretchen stamped *two* times. In spite of myself, I felt a grin blooming. Gretchen followed with a staccato of stamping, and then a war whoop, and finally launched into a full-fledged, very politically incorrect, parody of a Native American rain dance.

I couldn't help myself, I started to laugh. It didn't matter that I might have just signed my own death warrant. The idea of

Gretchen as Pocahontas was too, too funny. If *Gretchen* were to try to sing about the wind's colors, all the little forest animals for miles around would cower in their dens, with their little paws clamped to their ears to block the sound.

"Now that we have that settled," Travis chortled, "how do we find Thanatos' lair? Or do we sit here and wait for him to show up again?"

"I may not know much about anything important--" I started to say once I got my breath back.

"That's for sure."

"But I have instincts. And my instincts tell me that Thanatos is gonna come looking for me."

"How sure of that are these...instincts?" Gretchen wanted to know.

"I doubt there's much anyone could do to stop him."

They stood silently, waiting for me to explain. Enjoying having the upper hand for once, I waited for them while they waited. Eventually, all that waiting became too much for Gretchen and she cracked.

"Dammit, Alec. Spill, will you?"

"I speak from experience. I used to hustle, remember?"

"What *are* you talking about?"

It was my turn to look smug.

"That boy is just *dying* to get into my pants! Wild horses couldn't keep him away."

CHAPTER THIRTEEN

Normally, I would have raised hell about all the extra hours Peter was working. Between Thanatos' threats, the aftermath of the explosion at the Special Projects building, and Jackson Greene's health issues, my husband had his hands full. For once, I didn't mind. It was safer if Peter kept himself busy.

By day, I dealt with client problems and with Randy's moods. But as soon as twilight fell, the Whirlwind hit the streets, or the rooftops, to be more accurate. Down on the ground, the police were out in full force, even though Gretchen had agreed that it was unlikely they'd find Thanatos until he was good and ready to be found. In the meantime, I hoped that by making myself as visible as I could, I could lure him into showing himself.

It was impossible not to be flattered that a guy as hot as Thanatos was interested in me, even if he was a criminal. I confess that I was looking forward to our next meeting as well. I tried to alleviate my guilt by telling myself that it was only because I wanted to thwart his evil plan, but I wasn't fooling anyone. I knew that my attraction to Thanatos wasn't any worse of an infidelity to Peter than my casually cruising a hot stranger at the gym. So long as nothing happened, technically, I hadn't done anything wrong. Yet I felt very much like I *had* done something wrong. The sheer power of the animal lust I felt for the guy terrified me. I kept praying that our second meeting would prove the chemistry between us to be a fluke. At the same time, there was a not-so-silent part of me that was hoping it wasn't.

Maybe I was just in denial.

Crouched atop of the Centerport Courier Building, bored, and with the threat of rain in the air, I allowed my fantasies to get the better of me. What would Thanatos look like, I wondered, if he shed the costume and stood before me in all his naked, evil splendor? Would his chest be hairy or smooth? Would he have a tan line? Was the codpiece justified? Or was it wishful thinking on his part?

In spite of my wedding vows, I was understandably curious.

It wasn't that I wanted to have mind-blowing sex with the guy. I didn't. Okay, so maybe I did. But I had enough self-control not to. Still, even if I had no intention of following through, the desire to see him nude was making me crazy. From experience, I knew that being captured by a supervillain was not entirely out of the question; it had happened before. What if I found myself bound in chains while Thanatos loomed over my helpless body, all black leather and studly muscle? Could I rely on my hormones *not* to betray my better judgment?

"We've got problems."

Travis' voice boomed out of nowhere. Ever since he installed a headset in my mask, I'd been trying to ignore it. It was uncomfortable, like ear buds that don't quite fit, but never actually fall out. He claimed I'd get used to the sensation. So far, I hadn't. It was easy enough to forget about when we weren't using it. But the sound of a disembodied voice blaring in my ear without any warning was enough to startle me until I realized what it was. I spun around looking for the intruder, tripped over the cape, slid down the roof, and only stopped myself by slamming into the parapet just before I plummeted into Lincoln Avenue.

"Jesus, kiddo. You got a mouth on you. You sure as heck didn't learn that kinda language from me."

"Sorry, Trav. You caught me off guard and I had a little... incident."

"We got some little incidents here too. I just heard on the police band that they admitted a couple of Gretchen's people to Polk Medical Center. I only managed to get in a few words with her before she had to run. My sources tell me it's severe malnutrition."

"Shit."

"At least your language is improving. The good news…"

"*Dammit!*"

I'd cupped my ear to hear better, and the damned microphone came off in my hand. I held it up to my lips. "Could you repeat that?"

"It turns out that one of the Greene Genes botanists assigned to a completely different project was growing some of the tainted veggies on the sly. Seems she wanted a transfer onto Brad Harmon's team. Seeing as Brad's staff is all in a billion pieces, she's lucky she stayed where she is. Her crop isn't very big but there's enough mature produce to keep the victims alive until Greene Genes can synthesize the antidote. They're also continuing with Brad's work to try and develop yet *another* virus to try and halt the spread of Three-Two-Three in case Thanatos goes ahead and releases it. I tell you…" From his tone, I knew he was frowning and shaking his head. "…Damn that Jackson Greene and all his damned viruses. At his age, you'd think he'd know better than to mess around with stuff like that. Oh, his *intentions* were always good, I've no doubt about that. I just wish he would have taken a step back and thought about how one little mistake could turn the whole human race into a bunch of mutated monkeys."

"You got any ideas to help out?"

"I'm attacking it from the nanoprobe angle. That's right up my alley. If they find a cure, I'll make sure the delivery system… uh…shows up on their computer systems. But they're working from Brad's old notes and experiments. His more recent materials were destroyed. So, it'll take time."

"How many people got infected? *Mother humper!*"

"What's got your titties in an uproar?"

"It's this damned microphone. It keeps falling off. And *why* is there no volume control?"

"Would you listen if I whispered? I don't think so. Shouting is the only way to get your atten–"

"Hang on." I squinted against a light mist that had slowly crept over the roof. "I see something weird over by the Fillmore bridge. I'm gonna check it out."

"Keep me posted."

"Fat chance," I said. "I'm leaving this stupid headset on top of the Courier Building."

"Alec..."

"Don't you 'Alec' me. I'm done with this thing."

Before he could protest any further, I dropped the mechanism onto the roof, stepped on it, and savored the sound of plastic cracking. When I was satisfied that it was beyond even Travis' ability to repair, I headed toward the bridge. As I got closer, I saw a plume of turquoise smoke streaming from the top of one of the pylons. In spite of myself, I was touched by his thoughtfulness in using my personal color. Thanatos might be evil, but maybe he was also kind of sweet.

The Fillmore is one of those old-fashioned suspension bridges, with cables all over the place, so it was an easy climb up the pylon. When I got to the top, he was waiting for me. The devil mobile was nowhere to be seen, which was odd, because it must have taken him a few trips to lug all that stuff up there by hand. The top of the pylon was a flat area of about nine yards square. In the center, he'd spread a red-checked table cloth to better display a huge picnic basket, chock full of goodies. Thanatos himself held a champagne flute in one hand, and a classy looking bottle in the other.

"Care to join me, Whirlwind?" He toasted me and took a sip. "It's not as sunny as I would like for a picnic. But still..."

"Sorry. I don't drink on the job. Besides, I *know* what you do to food. I think I'll stick to salads and protein shakes. Not that I don't appreciate the thought."

"Pity." He took a second sip. "I can't share this particular bottle, of course. But there's another of the same vintage in the basket if you change your mind."

He sighed with what I thought might be true regret. There was something a little...off about him. He was just as attractive but I didn't feel that libidinous pull I'd fought against when we first met on top of the water tower. Had his body not flickered, I might never have figured out why.

"Hologram." I couldn't keep the admiration from my voice.

"Aww, you noticed."

He pouted, and his lips under the cowl were plump and a little moist from the wine. Very...kissable.

"Where's the projector?"

He wagged one finger at me. "A boy shouldn't reveal all of his secrets on a first date."

"Second."

"The first time was more of a Meet and Greet, wouldn't you say? But if you like..."

He smiled and even though he wasn't really there, I could feel my heart pounding in my chest.

"...we can call this the second date. And you *know* what they say happens on third dates, right?"

"What's that?"

"Second base."

He grinned and, in spite of myself, I grinned back. But I quickly got control of myself before things could get out of hand, not that I could do anything with a hologram anyway, and got back to business.

"Look, Thanatos. I'm not a cop. My job description doesn't demand that I bring you to justice, or make you pay your debt to society, or any of that crap. I'm strictly unofficial." He seemed to be listening so, emboldened, I continued, "My only concern is with protecting innocent people. Believe me, you have no idea what a pain in the ass that can be sometimes. So, I'm asking you...how about cutting me a little break? What do we say you just take a hike and give up all this extortion nonsense?"

I saw his fingers tighten on the champagne glass.

"I'm not going to try and convince you that'll be an easy choice for you to make. For one thing, there are already a bunch of cops in the hospital. Chief Thatcher is going to ream me a new one for not bringing her your head on a platter. That's not your concern; I'll find a way to deal with it. You strike me as a smart guy. If you forget about the money and go on your merry way, Captain Dirigible'll show up eventually, or the Aphid, and Gretchen will forget all about you. As for the Whirlwind," I shrugged. "I'm done. Once the threat is gone, you won't be my business any more. I won't give you another thought."

"Somehow, I doubt that," he said softly.

Suddenly my costume was way too tight in certain places. Again.

"Maybe you're right," I admitted, just as quietly. "Maybe someday we'll pass on the street, or we'll be sitting at opposite ends of a bar, or waiting for the same bus. I won't be in turquoise and you'll have ditched the leather. We won't even know each other. But then…"

"Our eyes will meet."

I nodded, my throat dry. "We'll smile."

"We'll *want* each other…"

"Sometimes," I said with not a little melancholia, "you have to be content with just the wanting."

"Ah," he said. "I see."

The wind picked up a little. Up so high, it can get pretty chilly. I suppose that was what made me shiver.

"You already have someone."

There was sadness in his voice and…something else. I knew what it was.

"So do you," I said.

After a pause, he nodded once, very slowly.

"All this flirting and chemistry aside," I told him, "I think we both know neither of us is going to risk losing that. No matter how…um…"

"Powerful."

"Yeah. No matter how powerful this *thing* is between us."

He thought it over. For a moment, I fooled myself into thinking I'd convinced him. But when he reached his decision, I already knew what it would be. It both disappointed and saddened me.

"If you knew why I need to do this, perhaps you'd understand. You would still try to stop me but you might consider forgiving me. As things are, though, I hope you know how reluctant I am to get rid of you."

"You can try." I tightened my muscles in preparation for something nasty.

"I've studied you. You're strong, fast, and able to take a lot of damage. But I'm fairly sure you're still human. Of course, everyone knows you feel pain."

I did not like where the conversation was headed.

"What do you mean 'everyone' knows I feel pain?"

He chuckled. "I don't think you realize how vocal you can be. Especially when you're not aware there's a news crew around."

My cheeks got very warm.

"I'm truly sorry," he said. "I need you out of the way. At least until I get my money. If it makes any difference, I really hope this doesn't kill you because...well...I'd feel very bad about that."

He set the champagne bottle down outside of the projector range. His hand vanished and, when it reappeared, he was holding a small box that was featureless except for a single button. Somewhat reluctantly I thought, he jabbed it with his forefinger.

Pain.

Excruciating pain.

Every muscle in my body contracted spasmodically and my nerves felt like they'd been replaced with molten wires. My back arched with agony, and my teeth slammed together so hard that I was convinced I'd be spitting enamel for a week.

"I would have preferred to share a picnic lunch with you. In the end, the blanket served its purpose. The grid's hidden underneath."

I was fighting to keep my spine from bursting out of the top of my head, and praying my testicles wouldn't simply explode. His words registered, dimly, but enough for me to understand that I needed to get *off* that damned picnic blanket. For some reason, I could not move an inch. My brain was fuzzy with the pain, and so it took me longer than it should have to realize why I was frozen in place. The sexy bastard was electrocuting me!

If I got out of this alive, I was going to have some serious words with Travis about altering my costume so it was a poor conductor. For now, though, I could see flickers of static shooting between my fingers and up my arms, tiny lightning bolts that danced across the surface of my skin. I looked like a turquoise version of the contraption that Dr. Frankenstein used to bring the Monster to life.

"Later, stud."

With that, the image vanished. The current, however, did not. It got worse. My muscles continued to spasm. My neurons kept misfiring. As if that wasn't bad enough, the clouds chose that moment to break open. The rain poured down and reminded me that it is generally not a good idea to mix water with electricity. Nature drove home her point with a light show of sparks, fizzles, and some more miniature lightning bolts, all of which came out of *my* body! I tried to lift my feet, and managed to kick the picnic basket instead. It soared over the edge of the platform and dropped toward the river. I couldn't even shuffle off the grid, the current held me too firmly in place.

Then, I got lucky.

Sort of.

Something blew up.

Later, I'd find out that the rain overwhelmed the grid and shorted the generator that Thanatos had stashed at the base of the pylon. In the moment though, all I knew was that a final jolt of electricity zapped me with enough juice to hurl me completely off the bridge. I barely had time to register that the pain was gone before I spied the picnic basket below me. It hit the river and burst asunder. Bits of the wreckage floated down the river. Unfortunately, since I was not made of wicker, presumably I was about to share the fate of the champagne bottle, which had either sunk straight to the bottom or was smashed to smithereens on impact.

Another swan dive was out of the question. Even if I'd thought of it in time, my nerves and muscles were still all a-jangle and refused to obey me. It probably wouldn't have helped much. The Fillmore is a pretty high bridge.

I plummeted down, with no way to stop myself, and with the water rushing toward me. I imagined that the impact was going to feel like slamming into a concrete parking lot.

I was wrong.

It felt like slamming into *three* concrete parking lots.

CHAPTER FOURTEEN

I vaguely remember thinking that a herd of buffalo were using my body as a trampoline. By the time my water-logged body surfaced, spewing filthy river water like a fountain, they'd all swum back to the prairie.

Someone spotted me floating down the river like the wreckage of a turquoise *Titanic*, and called 9-1-1. By the time Gretchen found out about it, I was halfway to the Polk Medical Center. In a purple panic, she called Travis. Somehow, he managed to intercept the ambulance, get me out of it, and spirit me back to Ale Mary's. I have a dim recollection of Travis carrying me up the stairs to my apartment above the bar, but my clearest memory of those few hours is wondering when my muscles decided to play a drunken game of Twister. I also seem to recall that Gretchen helped him strip me out of the costume and get me into bed.

If I'm lucky, that last part was a dream. I felt bad enough. The last thing I needed was Gretchen making smart ass comments about parts of my anatomy that she normally doesn't get to see.

When Peter came home, Travis told him I'd come down with a really bad flu. Normally, my husband would have waited on me like Florence Nightingale. But he'd just gotten word of Jackson's death and it floored him, even though he'd been expecting it. Jackson had no family so, as his protégée, Peter was expected to make all the arrangements. This was on top of trying to make sure the reigns at Greene Genes changed hands smoothly, and coping with whatever Thanatos planned to throw at Centerport next.

I suspect he was grateful to Travis for tending to me in my

sickroom; it was one less thing he needed to worry about, and he couldn't risk getting sick himself at such a crucial moment for the company. Even so, when I finally woke up, and could see without flashes of rainbow lights obscuring my vision, it was to a half dozen bouquets of fresh gladiolas and tuber roses. On the dresser was a stack of familiar white and gold marzipan boxes topped with a huge piece of cardboard upon which Peter had printed:

Not Until You Feel Better!

"He wanted to be here," Travis said. "I sent him back to work."

"But..."

"No buts. The flu story won't hold water–not nearly as much water as you spat up when they dragged you out of the river. I told him you're highly contagious. He'll be sleeping in the guestroom."

"Travis!" I wailed. Peter and I had never once slept apart since the week we met.

"I know, kiddo." He seemed genuinely sorry. "We can't risk him realizing what's really wrong with you. Your impersonation of a light bulb made the front page of the Courier. Do you want him to put two and two together?"

"No." I winced. "What *is* wrong with me, by the way? I've *never* been hit this hard, or felt like this."

"Electrocution."

"You're shitting me. I've been electrocuted before."

"No, you've experienced minor shocks before. Nothing this bad. It seems a high enough current shorts you out. It's the Whirlwind's version of Kryptonite, you might say."

"How the hell did Thanatos know *that*? Even *we* didn't know it."

Travis frowned and looked worried.

"If you think that doesn't bother the crap out of me, you can think again. We're going to have to figure it out later. In the meantime, I'll find a way to insulate the costume and..."

"There's no time for that. Help me up."

"Whoa there, pardner!" A beefy hand on my chest shoved me back onto the bed. "Your muscles are like jelly and your neurons are dancing the Watusi all over the place."

"Is that what's wrong with my fingers?" They'd been twitching involuntarily since I'd regained consciousness.

"Your fingers?" Travis snorted. "You should see the left side of your face."

He must have seen my look of dismay. I can be brave about being shot, stabbed, blown up, incinerated, lasered, doused with radiation, and almost anything else. But when it comes to possible disfigurement, I panic.

I'm vain. So, sue me.

"Relax. The swelling is subsiding. But you are down for the count. At least for a day or two."

"We have to stop Thanatos!"

"I'm aware of that. There have been some new developments as well."

"Oh? Do tell."

"Just before he died, Jackson told Peter that Brad Harmon kept copies of everything in a safe."

"Not to speak ill of the dead but Jackson came up with that revelation a little late, dontcha think?"

"Pete went directly from the hospital to Bradley's place. By the time he got there…"

"Don't tell me. The safe was open and the stuff was gone."

He looked glum. "Gretch and I can't figure out how Thanatos knew about it."

"Unless…argh!" When I tried to shift into a more comfortable position, a blast of molten lead attacked my muscles and I collapsed while every nerve in my body yelled in protest at the same time.

"Take it easy, Alec. I told you. It's gonna take a couple of days."

"In that case," I said through gritted teeth, "would you kindly lift the invalid so he has a view of something other than his tastefully painted ceiling?"

Once he'd propped me up, I wiggled my fingers gingerly. I didn't have much control but at least the effort didn't send spears of agony up my arms.

"You were saying?"

"I may not be able to move, but my mind still works. Jackson and Bradley were the only two who knew about the safe, right? Jackson sure as hell wouldn't tell Thanatos squat. Which means..."

Travis blinked. He blinked again. He looked like one of those animatronic bears at Disneyland.

"Bradley's alive?"

"That's what I'm thinking," I said. "Unless they found his body. Did they?"

Travis shook his head.

"The lab was a shambles. *None* of the bodies were intact. The bits and pieces are still being DNA tested so they know which relatives get what."

"Just suppose Brad wasn't killed. That he was kidnaped instead."

"Okay, I'm with you."

"It's *his* virus, right? If he's alive, he might be our best weapon against Thanatos. Besides, finding him will give me something constructive to do."

"What if they're in this together? Brad and Thanatos."

I shook my head before I remembered I wasn't supposed to do that. I was delighted that my skull didn't detach from my spine and roll across the floor.

"I can't see Bradley Harmon as a bad guy. Oh, he's arrogant enough. But he's a complete wimp. He doesn't have the balls to get involved in something like this. Besides, Thanatos and I connected..."

Travis snorted but I ignored him.

"I feel like I understand him on some kind of deeper level. I'm absolutely positive that he works alone."

"Are you *sure* that's not the little head talking? I mean..." His attention was fixed very intently on the wallpaper. "I know you'd never be unfaithful to Peter but...you're mighty attracted to him, aren't you?"

"Yeah," I confessed glumly. "I can't help it."

"You wouldn't ever...?"

"Travis Buttrick! You've gone and hurt my feelings! Up 'til

now, they were the only part of my body that didn't ache."

"*That's* a relief."

"I can still fantasize." I grinned wickedly. "So can Thanatos. And that's our edge."

"Huh?"

"Thanatos may have found that my weakness is electricity. Hopefully, he doesn't yet understand that I've also found his. Me."

"You may think you're a dynamite piece of ass, Alec. But no roll in the hay is worth twenty-seven million bucks."

"If Thanatos had to make a choice between the two, I'd agree. But once he knows I'm still alive, I think he'll make a play for both me *and* the money. The connection between us is that powerful."

"Yeah. Right," he scoffed.

"I'm not exaggerating. You know I'd never cheat on Peter. But I tell ya, Trav, you have no idea how tough it was for me not to rip the guy's armor off and go at it right on top of the water tower."

"Do you think maybe he's using pheromones against you?"

I considered it for a moment and then shook my head.

"I doubt it. The feeling goes both ways. I'm sure of it."

"If you're right…and if you can resist your urges better than he can…" His eyes gleamed. "…We have a weapon."

"We have a weapon," I agreed.

"Oh! Speaking of weapons, Gretchen slipped me some blood samples from the victims. With any luck, I should be able to isolate the nanoprobes. It's not much, but it will hopefully confirm our theories at least."

"What about a vaccine for the virus?"

"That's way above my pay grade," Travis said. "The good news is that now that I have the samples, you don't need to go out and get infected. Just in case Thanatos' tailor-made something specifically for your body chemistry, I don't want to risk it."

"Could he *do* that?"

"I have no idea. He knew about the electricity and *that* sure as hell caught me off guard."

"I was thinking the same thing while sparks were shooting

out of my butt. Speaking about things shooting out of my body..."

"Yeah?"

I struggled to swing my legs to the floor but they refused to respond.

"I...er..." My face grew hot as I wondered how to ask what I needed to ask without actually asking. "I need your help. With...you know?"

Travis wasn't getting the hint.

"I mean...because my legs are all wonky..."

"I haven't the foggiest..."

"Damn it! I have to pee!" I blurted.

"You don't honestly expect me to..." He was horrified.

"Just help me to the bathroom," I grumbled. "I can manage the other part all by myself."

CHAPTER FIFTEEN

There were no banks of computers, no hidden traps, no massive view screens, no missile consoles. There wasn't even a throne. There was only a plain wooden chair in the middle of a bare room, a simple folding table, and a laptop. Even the computer wasn't particularly sophisticated.

Thanatos sat in silence, staring at nothing. His thoughts were devoted to pondering what he should do about the dilemma he found himself faced with–the dilemma in the blue tights.

He had only a slight compunction against killing again. By the same token, he hoped it wouldn't be necessary. Unlike some of the other arch villains that had plagued Centerport, Thanatos did not believe in rampant destruction and mindless mayhem without reason. Nor did he think of himself as a bad man, merely as someone who was driven. Chaos and death, he believed, should be used sparingly, and only if they brought him closer to his goals. Needless cruelty was not his style but, if a few more murders would get what he wanted, so be it.

The need to eliminate the Whirlwind had always been a possibility. If you were going to be a criminal in Centerport, as villains like Destructo, Doctor Dire, and Erica the Eel had discovered to their undoing, you'd have to be an utter fool if you failed to plan against interference from the local hero. Thanatos despised people who meddled in other people's business, and the Whirlwind was certainly a first-class meddler. He had to be removed from the playing field.

And yet...

He hadn't counted on the intensity of the attraction between them. It bordered on overwhelming. Fifteen seconds after the

Whirlwind showed up in that ridiculously colored costume, Thanatos felt like a school girl, weak-kneed and waiting for the quarterback to ask her to the prom. How had the Whirlwind so effortlessly wormed his way under Thanatos' skin?

It was hard to deny the purely physical attraction. But that was mere lust; he had certainly overcome lust before. These feelings eclipsed even "chemistry." The Whirlwind's mere presence set Thanatos' thoughts and emotions spinning, spinning, spinning into a whirlwind.

With not a little reluctance, he concluded that the Whirlwind had to go. Even so, he could not help a certain distaste when it came down to the methods he'd have to use. He'd confirmed his suspicions that electricity was the hero's Achilles Heel, but he found it extremely distasteful to think about charring that perfect body to a crisp. If only he could think of a way to dispose of the pest while still preserving the Whirlwind's beauty. It was a pity that, as far as Thanatos knew, there was no such thing as a freeze ray. He'd have much preferred to freeze his nemesis in a block of ice so that he could look at him from time to time, and lose himself in what-might-have-beens.

He shuddered. His thoughts were becoming macabre. Enough of these ridiculous fantasies.

A more constructive use of his time would be to double-check that he'd covered his tracks. He could not risk his identity being revealed. Everything he'd worked for would be destroyed. Even the money wouldn't be able to patch things up.

Twenty-seven million.

He'd chosen that amount with great care. It was low enough that the city wouldn't balk too badly at paying it, yet large enough to take him away from Centerport. Only then would he be able to banish the memories of a wretched past that gnawed at his soul like a cancer. Managed carefully, it would more than suffice for their needs. Thanatos would never have to work another day in his life; more importantly, *neither* of them would have to work. The past couldn't be changed, of course, but with enough money, he could remove all evidence of it and never have to worry about its ugliness again.

But before any of that could come to pass, Thanatos needed

to eliminate the Whirlwind.

An idea was taking shape. The abandoned foundry would be the perfect place to do it. The traditional methods, however, would have to be altered; immersing something that was the size of the Whirlwind would be problematic. He seemed to recall that, at one point, Greene Genes had conducted some research into a similar process; with any luck, the necessary equipment would still be in storage. As for the raw materials, well, he wouldn't need much. They were required only for the final...*artistic* effect. The process itself would surely be enough to dispatch the Whirlwind.

It was of primary importance to be certain of his technique. Otherwise, he risked botching the whole thing. Fortunately, one could learn how to do just about anything on YouTube. He moved to the laptop and began to type out a query with two fingers.

Perhaps there was a way for him to hang on to the Whirlwind after all.

CHAPTER SIXTEEN

"Are you sure you're feeling well enough to go in to work? Can't Randy handle things?"

It was the third time Pete had asked. If it had been Travis or Gretchen, I would have snapped at them for mollycoddling me. Having Peter fussing over me felt nice.

"I'm fine."

I stumbled and fell against Peter's chest. Damn, he smelled good!

Every so often, an agency client will express interest in a fetish known as Man Smell. It rarely takes Sven, the big blond who does most of our specialty work, more than an hour of gym time to create an aroma pungent enough to satisfy even the most extreme afficionado of this particular fetish. Personally, I never understood the appeal of having sex with a guy who stinks like he hasn't showered since last January. Some guys *look* great with torsos shining with a sheen of sweat; but that's mostly in centerfolds and online profiles where you don't have to smell them.

And yet...

I can't deny the power of pheromones.

Back when I was hooking, it didn't matter how hot the guy was, or how much he was willing to pay, if he reeked of stale onions and old gym socks, I took a pass. On the other hand, the way some guys smell drives me wild. Peter is definitely one of them. It doesn't matter whether he's just home from the gym, fresh from the shower, or if he's been stuck in the same business suit all day, Peter always smells like fresh heather. Not foofy or flowery. But natural and clean, with a distinct undertone of maleness. Sexually, it drives me wild, but it's a comforting smell too. Whenever I'm having trouble sleeping, I just snuggle close enough to breathe Peter in, and I'm out like a light.

We both pass on colognes. We've shared enough locker rooms with guys who don't understand that Halston for Men isn't cheaper when you buy it by the gallon. It's terribly unattractive to smell like a flower patch in which a musk deer has vomited up a vanilla cupcake. Antiperspirant, on the other hand, is just good manners.

In any case, my injuries had kept us apart at night and since Pete was smelling especially delicious...

"Hey, none of that," he chided gently. "You may be feeling better, but you're still weak."

He guided me to a chair and eased me into it.

"I don't like this," he continued, "If anything comes up, Randy can pick up a phone. That's what you pay him for."

"I've taken enough time off already. The Belgians are arriving today. They drink very strong coffee and they're partial to very ripe cheeses, and lots of garlic and onions. Do you know how difficult it is to get the boys to work under those conditions? Randy's powers of manipulation are legendary. But there's nothing like being called into the boss's office to whip a recalcitrant hooker into shape."

Pete tried another tact.

"What if you're still contagious? You could infect your staff."

"I'll douse myself in Clorox and wear a welding mask."

My resolve wavered. I would have loved to spend the day curled up in bed next to him. But the Whirlwind needed to get back to work. I was convinced that the only way Thanatos could have known about the hidden safe was if Brad Harmon was still alive. And I'd meant what I'd told Travis; there was no way Bradley would have cooperated willingly. In all likelihood, he was being held hostage somewhere. For all I knew, all that black leather might not have been just for show and Thanatos might have tortured the information out of him. There were a lot of questions, but a few things were clear. I had to locate Bradley Harmon, rescue him, and get him started on undoing the damage he'd done.

In the meantime, I needed to convince Peter to let me leave the house.

"We have a kitchen at the agency and Randy can make chicken soup for me."

"Randy can cook?"

"He microwaves with reckless abandon. I'll tell you what…"

I also wanted to make sure that Peter wouldn't be calling my office every half hour to make sure I was okay, or worse, dropping by to check on me and discovering that I was gone.

"As soon as I'm finished setting up the Belgians, I will barricade my office, turn off the phones, take a pill and crash on the couch."

"Under warm blankets?"

"The souvenirs Jackson brought us from Mexico."

"Alec! Those are museum quality! Examples of indigenous culture! Weren't you going to have them mounted and framed?"

"I never got around to it. I know it'll be hard but please don't worry about me. I'm going to try and sleep and I don't need Randy to barge in half a billion times dressed like Florence Nightingale."

Pete shuddered. "Yeah. I can see how that might make you sicker. Still, I really wish…"

"Enough!" I put my index finger to his lips to quiet him. He sucked on it, playfully. "The Belgians will be here for two weeks and they're paying top dollar. I want to get them started out on the right foot. As soon as I'm sure there are no complications, I'll let Randy take over. Besides, how long have we been meaning to rip out that crappy carpet downstairs and fix the parquet underneath? With the fees from this gig, we can afford to start converting the nightclub so that we have a decent sized living room for a change."

"Go on then," he said. "But I don't have to like it."

"So long as you still love me…"

Peter surprised me by sweeping me into an embrace so tight that, had I been a normal human, he would have bruised my ribs. He pressed my face into his shoulder and buried his in my hair.

"Oh, Alec," he whispered. "If you only knew how much."

When he broke the clinch, not releasing me but putting just enough space between us to let me breathe again, he had tears in his eyes.

"The only thing I want in this whole world is to make you happy. I know you think I worry too much, but if God forbid something ever happened to you..."

His tears spilled over. My own eyes grew moist.

"I don't know what I'd do. My job at Greene Genes is important but you...you're my whole life."

Smiling through his tears, he continued with almost frightening intensity.

"Please forget about that stupid agency for once. I'll skip work, too. We can both stay home. It'll be like a mini stay-cation."

"What about Jackson's funeral? All the lawyers? The insurance people?"

"Deborah Macintosh can deal with it. Herman would prefer me not to be around anyway. We can spend all day in bed. No sex, if you're not up to it. We'll just hold each other and think about how lucky we are. How about it?"

"No," I whispered. "We can't. Not today. We have responsibilities. Both of us do."

His arms tightened around me for a brief instant. Then, he let go.

"Soon? Promise me?"

"Wild horses couldn't stop me from keeping that promise."

His face lit up. "You'd better."

He kissed me again and left for work. As the door closed behind him, I had a last glimpse of the back of his head, hair still slightly damp from the shower. A horrible chill washed over me, an ominous frisson from out of nowhere. I almost called out to him. I wanted to tell him I'd changed my mind. But I knew I couldn't. I shivered, though it wasn't cold. I sat on the bed and drew my legs into my chest, wrapped my arms around my knees, and couldn't stop shaking.

I told myself that it was nothing worse than a side effect from the stress of the past few days. I had no other explanation for the horrible, irrational sense of dread that whispered to me that I would never see my husband again.

CHAPTER SEVENTEEN

"I'm telling you, he won't do it."

While I'd been home recovering from my injuries, Randy had been experimenting with blond highlights. His normally ebon tresses looked like a slice of tuxedo cake. The bizarre visual effect made it very difficult for me to concentrate on what he was saying.

"They're paying more than triple his usual rate," I growled. By this point in the conversation, I had no need to feign a headache.

"He says the thing with the rubber raft is too twisted."

"It's a *fetish*, you dizzy queen. It's *supposed* to be twisted."

One of my boys, Lance, had refused a date with one of the Belgians. Normally, we could have simply sent a different guy. Monsieur Tremblanc, however, had a crush on Lance and was willing to pay through the nose for him.

"It's not *just* the raft. God *knows*, Lance had done far kinkier things. Did you *see* that video he made? Who knew you could do *that* with cottage cheese? And the bit with the Ficus tree? Our Lance is *truly* inspired when the impulse strikes."

"What's the problem then?" I longed to end this conversation, and not just because I needed to suit up and get busy.

Randy lowered his voice as if confiding a secret.

"It's the wiener dogs. Lance says they creep him out."

"Oh, for Christ's sake!" I finally exploded. "It's not like they *participate*! They stay in the damned cage."

"They watch," he said, smugly, as if that settled the matter. "What's worse is...Lance *swears* they lick their lips."

"Dogs can't actually do that, can they?"

"When they see that much ground meat, they do. Tremblanc

isn't a small man. Last time, it took thirty pounds of sausage."

"Which we made a profit on as well," I pointed out.

"Not after Tremblanc let the dogs out and the greedy little monsters gobbled up what was left over and got sick. Deep cleaning hotel carpeting is *not* cheap."

"He reimbursed us."

"Four months later."

"Tell Lance," I said. "If he does this, I'll move him to the front of the line for the next time Chet Herrington comes to town. Last year, Chet flew David to Hawaii for the weekend."

"That might do it." He pursed his lips while he was thinking things through. "Yes, I think he'd go for that."

I breathed a silent sigh of relief. "Make it so. While you're at it, hold all my calls. I've got a headache to beat the band."

"Even calls from Peter?"

"Especially from Peter. Tell him I'm napping and I threatened to rip that dye job out by the roots if you wake me."

"I'll have you know that Terrence at Mein Lieber Hair did it. It took me *months* to get an appointment."

"God made you a brunette for a reason," I said. "And your eyebrows defy His Divine Will. What color *is* that? Goldenrod? Lemon Chiffon? Banana Creme Pie?"

"It's *all* the rage," he pouted.

"Maybe for an elf on crack," I said.

"Go ahead," he yelled over his shoulder as he flounced out in a huff. "Insult the help if it makes you feel like a big man."

"No calls!" I yelled after him.

Five minutes later, I was good to go. Travis had come up with several lists of all the places in and around Centerport where a research scientist might be held hostage. The first list was depressingly long until we realized that, if Thanatos had kept Brad Harmon alive, it was because he needed the doctor's expertise. Bradley would, in turn, need certain resources in order to work, chief among them being reliable internet access capable of handling large amounts of secure data. Since ISPs rarely run cables into abandoned subway stations or the sub-basements of defunct factories, we were able to narrow the options substantially.

One location stood out.

The old Tellmore Lighthouse loomed over a high bluff about a quarter of a mile north of where the Fillmore river emptied into the sea. It was a popular picnic spot until the cliffs just below it began to collapse from erosion. The building was so rickety and dangerous that even high school kids looking for a place to shack up or smoke weed didn't dare risk breaking in. Travis found it very curious, therefore, when the Centerport Public Utility Company's records revealed that the water and power were still turned on. Digging a little deeper, he found that the bills were paid by a subsidiary of Greene Genes. The final straw, however, was when he found that someone had gone to the trouble of installing fiber optic internet in a lighthouse which was, supposedly, condemned.

It didn't take rocket science to conclude that we'd found *a* bad guy. The only question was whether or not it was *our* bad guy. After all, Centerport was not Thanatos' exclusive stomping ground.

Of course, it was always possible that some desperate, and possibly insane, real estate developer had decided to convert the lighthouse into quaint condo units. I scotched that option within seconds of my arrival. I took one look at the place and the words "wreck," "shambles," and "bulldozer" were the ones that most readily sprang to mind.

I circled the building, wary of any suspicious picnic blankets. The shiny new padlock on the rear door was yet another give-away. There were no security cameras and no visible alarms either. If this was the place where Doctor Harmon was stashed, it looked like Thanatos had been banking on our being unable to find him, rather than worrying about what would happen if we did. That kind of thinking smacked of over-confidence, or just plain sloppiness. I wasn't sure which possibility troubled me the most.

Before I entered, just to make sure that he wasn't going to spring a bunch of leather-clad minions on me at the last minute, I closed my eyes and engaged my proximity sense. The place didn't feel very occupied. Nevertheless, I got the sense of at least one presence inside the lighthouse that had more intelligence than a stray raccoon or squirrel that might be nesting in the battered stone walls.

The lock was a cinch. Unlike what they show on TV, they don't actually crumble into powder when you squeeze them. But if you grab the hasp and twist hard enough, they generally snap open. The door itself was metal, sturdy and had no discernable knob, although there was a little panel with numbers set into the shadows of the door frame.

Oh joy, an electronic lock.

In retrospect, it made sense. Given how tightly Thanatos' costume fit him, there wasn't much room for him to carry a set of keys. If I'd let Travis come along with me, he'd have been in his element. He loves any opportunity to use his gizmos, whether it's to bypass locks, or to eavesdrop on government agencies. He'd have happily fussed around with his wires and gadgets until he came up with the combination.

I don't have that kind of patience.

So, I just ripped out door.

Frame and all.

And left it propped against the stone wall next to the doorway.

The corridor was dark, and as dank as you'd expect the hallway in an abandoned lighthouse to be. There was no light switch. Just in case Thanatos was an afficionado of late-night infomercials, I clapped my hands once, softly. Still, no light.

Most of the doors on either side of the hallway were ajar. At one point, the rooms they revealed had been used as living space for the lighthouse keeper and his family. Now, they were empty of everything except ruined furniture, broken glass, used condoms, and miscellaneous junk. My muscles were still a little dicey, and a battered sofa tempted me to rest for a minute, but the stench of mildew and the furry critter that ran across one of the torn pillows made me reconsider. At the end of the passage, I found a landing with one long stairway going up, and one even longer going down. I looked for a third one, the one that went nowhere just for show. But there were only the two.

I had no need of my proximity sense to detect the waves of despair percolating up from the lower stairwell. The feeling of hopelessness that pervaded the place was almost palpable. Down I went, hugging the wall like a horror movie heroine creeping into the basement where the disembodied limbs of her fellow summer campers were stored. The stairs dead-ended at a small landing, with stone walls broken only by a single door sheathed in layers of sheet metal. The space seemed even more claustrophobic because the only light was from a single, low-wattage bulb, set high up on the wall, behind a protective mesh grill.

Gently, I tested the door and found to my surprise that it wasn't locked. Though it swung open easily enough, it scraped against the stone floor of the room within. I winced at the noise and, before it could alert anyone, I stepped inside.

My initial impression of the place was that Doctor Frankenstein could *really* use a maid service. There were a couple of heavy tables bolted to the floor, littered with scientific apparatus. The largest one was covered with beakers and burners, flasks and petri dishes, test tubes and microscopes, all scattered willy-nilly without any sense of organization or order. A few glass containers lay on their sides in puddles of whatever had spilled out of them.

The second table held half a dozen machines with glowing screens. One of them was a desk top computer; I had no idea what the other ones were for. As far as I knew, they could have been doing anything from tracking satellites to smog checking Thanatos' car. Post-It notes almost completely obscured a couple of the screens, and more paper, mostly full sheets, was taped to almost every vertical surface. It was as if whoever worked there needed to be able to see a written summary of every single thought he'd ever had, no matter how minor, all at the same time. Crumpled balls of paper littered the floor and there was a spray of broken glass where someone had tossed a container at the garbage can, missed, and hadn't bothered to clean it up.

A heavily padlocked cabinet was soldered to the near wall, wedged between a household refrigerator and a commercial freezer that was large enough to hold half a cow. Aside from the dim glow from the few unobstructed computer screens, the only light sources were a couple of overhead fixtures with faulty florescent bulbs that flickered and popped, alternately bathing the room with a harsh and chemical light, and plunging it into deep gloom. The strobe effect caused me to mistake the mound against the far wall for a pile of rubbish until, with a distinct clanking of chains, it moved.

"Whirlwind?" The voice was both exhausted and relieved.

Though I'd never known Bradley Harmon all that well, the distinctive whine in his voice was as memorable and as abrasive as the scrape of steel cutlery on stoneware dishes. "Grating" was an apt description of the sound. While he wasn't someone you might want to speak to at a social event unless you'd brought along a healthy dose of aspirin for the inevitable headache, in this case, the irritating quality in his voice was a boon. Otherwise, given his current condition, it would have been a stretch for me to have identified him by sight alone.

Not to mince words, the good doctor looked like shit.

Bradley was the typical absent-minded professor, albeit far more arrogant and impatient than most, so the rumpled clothing and cheek stubble wasn't unexpected. He was the type that, even at the best of times, often forgot to shower and shave for a few days because he was too absorbed in his work. Now, however, Harmon had been wearing the same Hawaiian shirt for so long that the outlines of the hula girls had bled into the rest of the pattern. Had it not been for the palm fronds all over the thing, I'd have thought the shirt was decorated with dancing turnips.

The only reason he wasn't corpse-pale was probably that he'd been kidnaped under the bright sun of Tahiti. Even so, the remnants of his tan bathed his complexion in a sallow cast, and his skin was the color of an unbaked lump of dough that had gone bad. His eyes were deeply hollowed, dark with fatigue, and desperate, and his hair was greasy and disheveled, as if Albert Einstein had plugged his finger into an electric socket.

And he stank. Good Lord, how he stank!

Bradley seemed to perspire a lot for someone who seemed as allergic to doing anything physical as I knew he was. The armpits of his filthy lab coat were stained yellowish brown. Only heaven knew what the underarms of the dancing vegetable shirt looked like underneath it. In any case, it was clear that he hadn't been allowed to bathe since his capture. Aside from the body odor, there was the scent of something unwholesome and fetid in the air; the shackle locked around his leg had chafed, and there was a large, festering wound on his ankle, leaking puss. It looked like a pit bull had chewed on his foot and smelled like a rancid compost heap."

"Oh, thank God! Thank God!" He kept repeating it.

He buried his face in his hands, weeping uncontrollably, while I stood awkwardly, trying not to gag on the stench and waiting for him to get control of himself. To his credit, the waterworks didn't last long.

"Quickly!" he pointed. "That cabinet. On the top shelf. You'll find a rack of vials."

I tore the door off the locked cabinet and located the proper stuff. When I handed it to him, I made sure to stand as far back as I could, and breathe through my mouth. To my surprise, he prepared a hypodermic and rolled up his sleeve.

"Um...I don't want to be judgmental but do you really want to be doing that now?

"Huh?" He expertly injected orange goo into his veins and dropped the empty syringe to the floor.

"I just think...I mean, we still have to get out of here. It'll help if you're not completely stoned when we do it."

"Stoned?" he snapped. "What nonsense is...? Oh! You meant..."

He started to laugh and, in a way, it was worse than the weeping. It was high-pitched and bordered on hysteria. At least it seemed to release some of his tension.

"I'm not an addict."

"Of course not," I agreed amiably. "Because given a choice between escaping and shooting up, you naturally chose..."

"I was poisoned, you idiot!"

He riffled through some of the ubiquitous paper, casting most of it aside until he found what he wanted. He rolled it into a tube and stuffed it into the pocket of his lab coat.

"The antidote's only temporary. But we have no time to worry about that now. Has that *horrible* man released the stuff yet?"

I nodded.

"Damn! Then we'll need these as well."

He quickly poured a measure from several different beakers into a small collection of plastic test tubes, capped them, and skillfully labeled them with a permanent marker.

"Oh! And this, of course..."

He grabbed a small box full of microscope slides.

"I almost forgot..."

He snatched a handful of flash drives and stood with his lab coat pockets bulging, tapping his uninjured foot impatiently.

"Well...?"

He waggled his cuffed leg.

"Are you planning on doing something about this? Or should we wait until Thanatos shows up and kills us both?"

Scowling while holding my breath, I snapped the cuff. He didn't bother to thank me.

"We must get to Greene Genes right away!" He waddled past me to the door.

"Are you sure about that? How do you feel if I asked you to take a little stroll through a through a car wash on our way?"

He paused, sniffed at his own armpit, made a face and seemed to consider the suggestion. Then he shook his head, shot me a poisonous glare and trudged up the stairs.

When we emerged from the lighthouse, Doctor Harmon stopped to stand blinking in the murky light. Tears ran down his cheeks and I half expected him to drop to his knees and kiss the ground.

"The sun! I thought I would never see the sun again."

"You're not seeing it," I pointed out helpfully. "It's overcast. Looks like we're due for another storm."

He gave me another poisonous look, followed by an abrupt, "Where's your car?"

"Car? What car? I walked. Well, I ran actually."

"I am by no means in any condition to run," he snapped. "Time is of the essence. You're going to have to carry me."

"You're kidding, right?"

"I am most certainly not kidding. It's essential I get these samples to a decent lab as soon as possible. Unless you *want* people to die?"

"But..."

My nose must have wrinkled because he understood my objection right away.

"*You* try being chained up in a dank dungeon for as long as I was and see how rosy *you* smell."

"You could have licked yourself clean," I offered. "Like a cat."

With a sigh of defeat and a silent reminder to myself *not* to inhale through the nostrils, I slung the scientist over my shoulder in a modified fireman's carry. Once I was sure his bulk was balanced correctly, I broke into a trot. Harmon grunted every time his mid-section jolted against my elbow.

"Do you...have to...be so...*rough?*" he gasped.

I ignored him.

"Are you sure you don't want to go to a hospital first? Or to the police? Maybe a quick dip in a Jacuzzi full of bleach?"

"Greene Genes."

You had to admire the guy's sense of purpose.

"Oh shit!"

"What now?" I asked.

Harmon was facing backwards, so he had a clear view of what was behind us.

"He's coming back! Faster, dammit! Run faster!"

I risked a peek. Sure enough, there was a black dot in the sky that resolved itself into Thanatos on his scooter as it loomed closer.

"You're not exactly a waif-like sylph," I growled. "The next time Weight Watchers slips one of those free trial coupons under your door, you might want to think things through before you toss it."

Harmon kicked his feet, presumably to urge me to greater speed. Instead, I lost my grip, and his portly ass tumbled to the ground with an audible "Oof!"

I didn't bother to collect him; there wasn't enough time. I spun, prepared to do battle with *both* my nemesis and my own libido once again.

"Into the woods," I ordered the scientist.

"What?"

"The woods, you idiot. Hide! I'll keep him occupied while you escape. The road's not far. Flag someone down. Promise to buy 'em a year's supply of air freshener."

"You want me to *walk*? I'm not wearing shoes!"

"Walk. Run. Skip. Gavotte. I don't care. Just...*go!*"

My urgency finally penetrated and Harmon stopped arguing. He half-limped and half-scurried into the trees. He vanished from sight just in time to miss Thanatos' far more graceful landing.

"What have we here?"

For a supervillain whose secret lair had been compromised, whose kidnaped scientist had been freed, and whose dastardly plans were about to be ruined, he seemed quite jolly.

"I guess coming along quietly is out of the question?" I asked.

He laughed, and I only just managed to catch myself before I joined in. No matter how attractive he was, I needed to remember that he'd tried to flash fry me without benefit of a pan.

"I was hoping to see you again, Whirlwind," he chuckled.

"I need to check my schedule. I might be able to squeeze you in for a coffee date. How does the first Wednesday after twenty-to-life work for you?"

"Cute," he said. "But even as cute as you are..."

In hindsight, my not being prepared for what came next seems incredibly stupid. Not that I'd abandoned all caution; I'd been alert the whole time. From the moment I'd entered the lighthouse, I'd been wary of where I put my feet lest I step on another concealed power grid. Even when I paused before kicking down that steel dungeon door, it was because I suspected that Thanatos might have it wired.

I never anticipated he'd have something portable.

The weapon just appeared. In his hand. Out of nowhere. I didn't even have time to flinch. I felt a sharp, stinging pain near my collarbone. Half a second later, all of my nerve cells were dancing on hot coals again.

Been there. Done that. Have the memories of lungs full of river water to prove it.

"Sorry," he said. "I turned up the voltage this time. Just to make sure. I hope you don't mind."

I had news for him. I minded.

My muscles turned into Spam, and I remained conscious just long enough to taste the dirt when my face slammed into the ground.

CHAPTER EIGHTEEN

"Where the hell could he be?"

Gretchen shrugged, her face twisted with worry. "We went to the Tellmore place and found everything just like Bradley described. Except…"

"Except?"

"No Whirlwind."

"Boogers," Travis cursed softly.

The two of them had stolen a few minutes away from the chaos surrounding Doctor Harmon's reappearance by ducking into a storage closet. Fortunately, the Polk Medical Center kept a lot of spare everything on hand and the closets were large, so there was enough space for Travis's bulk. Unfortunately, there was very little space left over for the police chief. The two were pressed against each other, virtually chest-to-chest. Had anyone opened the door, they would have assumed they had interrupted a romantic tryst.

"You're sure he's not at the agency?" Only a faint trace of hope colored her voice; she already knew the answer.

"He told Randy he was napping. 'Do not disturb upon pain of death.' You know how dramatic he gets. Randy finally barged in anyway and Alec was gone. I double checked their apartment at Ale Mary's, and then I called Peter."

Gretchen winced. "I can't imagine that went well."

"I got lucky. His secretary said he was still at lunch."

Gretchen tiredly scrubbed her face with her hands. "At least we didn't find a body. Alec is hard to kill so, odds are, Thanatos is holding him somewhere."

"When Peter gets home tonight and finds Alec missing…

Damn! I *knew* I should have made insulating that suit a priority!"

Travis looked like he was frustrated enough to bang his forehead against the storeroom wall. Fortunately for the wall, it was covered with shelving.

"You had other things to worry about," Gretchen soothed. "Like saving innocent lives."

"Alec is innocent, too."

"He's only one person. If Thanatos gets impatient or decides to give us another demonstration, your work on the nanoprobes could help dozens, maybe hundreds. You done good, my friend. Besides, the Whirlwind's been captured before."

"True. But this business with Thanatos is different. It worries me. No one else ever suspected that electricity was the Whirlwind's weakness. Even *I* didn't know that! It's like this guy's got an inside line on information that no one else has."

"What can I do to help?"

"When Peter shows up, keep him occupied. Use any excuse to keep him from finding out Alec's missing. Arrest him if you have to."

"Arrest him?"

"Well, maybe not arrest him. Maybe you could drag him downtown for...I don't know...for questioning or something. People *died* at Greene Genes, Gretch. Pete's the acting Chairman of the board. There's got to be some kind of paperwork you can tie him up with for a few hours."

"I'll figure it out. Wait!" Her eyes glinted when she thought of something. "Didn't you once mention a homing device in Alec's suit?"

Travis grimaced. "I made the mistake of putting it into the earpiece. The kid was always bitching that it didn't fit and... well..." He reached into his pocket and pulled out a mangled hunk of plastic. "He got all huffy and took it off. Stepped on it too, it looks like." He smiled, sad but affectionate. "Typical."

"In the meantime, if we find Whirlwind, we find Thanatos. I've got every cop I can spare out looking. It's just a matter of time."

"I know," he replied miserably. "I just wish we had a better idea of how much time we have to spare."

CHAPTER NINETEEN

When I came to, I had a momentary hallucination that I was in the steam room at the gym. Though I was sweating like a pig, the illusion was foiled because I was fully dressed. In fact, the costume was virtually plastered to my skin by my own perspiration.

It slowly dawned on me that no steam room I'd ever been in had been quite so hellish. True, there was that same "hot air" smell all around, but it lacked the distinctive overtones of toasted menthol and over-heated chemical disinfectant that you find in most gym saunas. I tried to sit up, but the temperature was enervating, and I felt drowsy and weak.

It was only when I struggled in earnest to rise that I discovered that I was pinioned at the wrists and ankles, fixed in place by a very thin, very sturdy, strap around my chest. As the fog evaporated from my brain, I also noticed that my entire body was experiencing a tingling sensation that set my nerves on edge. I immediately understood that, even if I had the strength to snap the bindings, I'd still be caught in an electrical field.

My vision slowly swam into focus, though the electricity delayed that process quite a bit. Eventually, with a disproportionate amount of effort, I was able to turn my head slightly to look around. What I saw was not encouraging.

I was flat on my back at the bottom of a cavernous space, a huge factory with metal catwalks that bisected the open space high above me, crowned by a roof supported by steel beams that shimmered in the heat. I could see, as well as hear, a line of roaring furnaces stretching into the distance to my left.

Opposite them, a row of giant cauldrons large enough to hold double-sized portions of elephant stew bubbled and simmered, filled with molten metal.

Oh, great. Roasted alive. Again. How original.

The Aphid had tried it once, without much success. During the process, I'd been in agony. Nevertheless, I'd emerged relatively unscathed except for a weeks-long lingering sunburn that no amount of aloe vera could soothe. If that was what Thanatos had in mind, I didn't relish revisiting the experience.

Fully alert now, I realized that the throbbing hum that I'd assumed was part of the mechanical process of the furnaces was actually coming from inside my own head. The instant it registered on my consciousness, a headache blossomed. The noise from all the burbling, clanking, simmering, and creaking machinery was trying to convert it into a full-fledged migraine. It was a dull pain, rooted deep inside my skull, accompanied by very strong nausea. I dry-swallowed a few times to keep my gorge down. On my back as I was, trapped and unable to move, vomiting would not have been a good idea.

As if all that wasn't bad enough, there were an alarming number of abandoned tools within my immediate view. On second thought, they were more like "implements," as in "implements of torture." Clamps and shears and picks and other objects with sharp edges were scattered all over the place, as if the workers had dropped them in a hurry and fled. Not being a particularly handy type myself, I didn't know what most of them were supposed to be used for. But given that they were probably designed to rip through metal and to withstand molten heat, I had no doubt they could be easily re-purposed to cause a great deal of agony to tender Whirlwind skin.

The air was dusty and thick. Everything smelled horribly, horribly *hot*; that was the only way to describe it. It wasn't a particularly appealing smell but, looking on the bright side, it was a welcome relief from having to inhale Bradley Harmon's body odor. I sneezed.

"You're awake. Good. We can begin."

Those are not the words one wants to hear when one is vulnerable and tied to a table, no matter how hunky the speaker may be. One prefers something more akin to, "You just lay back, enjoy yourself, and let me do all the work."

I tried to speak. I'd like to think I would have uttered utter something noble and heroic, albeit cliched, like, "Do what you will! I'll resist you to the bitter end!" But the electric current made my mouth feel like it was filled with a wad of couch stuffing, and I couldn't get my tongue to move properly. All that came out was a garbled grunt.

"Eloquent," Thanatos observed.

He ran one finger slowly down the center of my chest, across my stomach, and stopped just short of the Happy Place before he moved outside of my range of vision. He fussed with something on a table and, when I heard the clatter of tools, I tensed my muscles as well as I could to prepare myself for impending torture.

"It's a shame. Splayed out like a juicy side of beef. Seems a pity not to take advantage, doesn't it?"

His meaning was clear and, to be honest, not completely objectionable. Much to my surprise, I discovered that there was at least one part of my body that was immune to the electric field. Evidently, Thanatos saw it too."

"I hate to disappoint you, but rape is not on the menu."

Before meeting Peter, I would have been drooling at the prospect. Now though, I was just drooling. Mostly because my saliva glands were screwy from the electricity as well.

"I hope you don't mind that I had to take off my cape."

He stepped forward so that I could see him again. There was something about the way he was standing that seemed odd. Then, it hit me.

The arrogant bastard was *posing*! His back was arched slightly to make his chest seem even bigger, and he was standing with one leg slightly turned out to better display his thigh muscles. The clincher was the way he kept flexing both his biceps, not enough to be overtly obvious, but enough to make his arms bulge. Not that I'd had any doubts since our *tete a tete* on the water tower, but I again saw how easy it was to be tricked into thinking he wore body armor.

"It sometimes gets in the way when I'm involved in more delicate operations."

Delicate operations?

I wasn't sure I liked the sound of that. Being tortured was kind of my stock in trade. Ever since the Whirlwind first came on the scene, one bad guy or another had been trying to kill him, and there seemed to be an unspoken competition to see which of them could come up with the most bizarre, or painful, way to do it. So, it wasn't like I wasn't used to the idea. But when he said "delicate operations," I got this weird feeling, like he was going to extract a few of my internal parts and sell them to Central American organ smugglers.

"Also, it's muggy in here."

Muggy? Thanatos was a master of understatement. I'd have chosen words like stifling, searing, and blistering. Although, since it was very possible that my skin and those adjectives might become better acquainted in a very few minutes, perhaps muggy was just a dandy way to put it.

"And the cape doesn't breathe very well."

That made two of us.

He ceased his flexing and came closer. In one hand, he held an opened container that looked a lot like a quart-sized paint can.

"I wouldn't confess this to just anyone, you understand. But I'm susceptible to heat rash." He winked behind the mask. "It's a very unattractive condition."

Who was he kidding? Unattractive? Thanatos could have posed for a centerfold even if he'd had leprosy.

He loomed over me and, for an instant, I thought maybe he'd reconsidered the not-taking-advantage part. Sadly, his intentions were much different.

"Look," he said, and there was a new quality to his voice, a regret that sounded very sincere. "I *know* you felt the same way I did when we met. Please believe me that if there was any other way but this..."

He stopped. If he hadn't been a lunatic about to try and kill me, I'd have sworn that he'd gotten a little choked up.

"I'm *not* evil," he said. "Not like those others. Not like that old lady who melts people and that crazy guy with the blimp."

"Captain Dirigible," I tried to say. But it came out sounding more like "Cuppin' Thimble".

"I really need you to understand that. I don't want you to die thinking that I'm just another bad guy."

It was kind of sweet in its own psychotic kind of way. However, as I quickly reminded myself, there were many, many other ways of showing someone how sweet you could be. In fact, freeing the hero and letting him live would be, I thought, an excellent way to demonstrate some sweetness.

"The truth is, if there was any way to make this easier for you, I would."

He dipped his fingers into the jar, scooped up a glob of something, and plopped it onto the center of my chest.

"At least this first part won't hurt at all."

He was right about that. In fact, as he continued to cover my chest with the goo, working it over my arms, and smoothing it onto my stomach and lower parts, I found myself thinking that, as massages go, this probably wasn't a bad one at all. Of course, it would have been a lot more pleasurable if I had some feeling left in my body. With *that* thought, a different one occurred to me:

What he'd said about the first part not hurting was troublesome.

What about the second part?

Or the third?

As he continued to spread the goo, I tried to struggle. It accomplished nothing other than some sympathetic, soothing noises from him. I think he thought he was helping me not to be afraid of dying. He had no idea how wrong he was.

I'd always known that the Whirlwind's career could be cut tragically short without much warning. I'd dealt with the possibility of my own death a long time ago and, to be frank, it didn't bother me much. I have always been, as one *Courier* reporter once wrote after an interview that hadn't gone nearly as well as it should have, a "reluctant" hero. The Whirlwind's death was no biggie, as far as I was concerned. I'd have gladly hung up the turquoise tights in favor of a normal life with Peter. It was only my damnable sense of responsibility and, let's face it, guilt, that made me continue with the Whirlwind *schtick*.

Before now, I'd had no doubt that, whatever awful fate Erica, or the Aphid, or Doctor Dire had planned for me, the Whirlwind would always find a way to triumph. But this predicament with Thanatos was different. I could see no way out. Death seemed inevitable. For the very first time, it occurred to me that, if the Whirlwind perished, Alec Archer was equally as doomed. To my surprise, no matter how bravely the Whirlwind was ready to face his fate, the Alec part of me was a wreck.

Death is death is death. When it happens, there's not a whole lot you can do about it. It was the thought of never seeing Peter again, of not being able to make sure he knew how much I loved him, of not being able to apologize for hiding such a big part of my life from him, even if it was only to keep him safe...*that* was the unbearable part. Alec Archer was a gibbering, blubbering mess, ready to beg, to plead, to bargain, to do *anything* if only he could avoid death and give him the chance to be with his husband again.

But the Whirlwind part of me weighed in as well. As much as Whirlwind grumbled about having to do what he did, he always took a certain pride in wearing the mask. And the mask was still in place. Pride, I guess, helped make him a lot stronger than Alec. And not just physically.

Even so, it was a struggle for me. The only way to keep the screaming young man inside me from being unleashed was to concentrate on something else. The electric field held me paralyzed; finding a way to shut it down seemed impossible. Given that escape was not an option, I concentrated on Thanatos himself, not just because he was so damned beautiful, but because it distracted the Alec part of my mind from thinking about whatever Fate had in store.

"It's traditional, I believe, to tell the hero exactly how he's going to die."

He leaned over me and the reflected flames from the furnaces glinted off the makeup under the mask, distorting the color of his irises even further. I don't know if it's common for people who are facing death to obsess about trivial things, but I felt a weird compulsion to learn the true color of Thanatos' eyes. It had suddenly become the most important thing in the universe for me.

"Do you know how stunning you are?" he whispered to me. "From the beginning, I struggled with what to do about you. I always felt destroying something so beautiful would be a crime."

Right. Like contaminating innocent people with a fatal virus was *not* a crime?

"It complicated my plans, and made things a lot more difficult for me. But I finally came up with a way of preserving your looks."

He fetched a heavy rolling cart. The boxy machinery on top had a wand attachment that reminded me a lot of an airbrush, or a tattoo needle. It was attached to something like looked like an air compressor.

"Greene Genes technology." He patted the machine with affection. "Usually, you need to immerse the...um...object in a salt solution. For more intricate work, you can use an inert gas. But since human flesh is a very poor conductor, I'll need to keep the current running through your body throughout the entire procedure. Unfortunately, it will take a while."

He sighed, and I sensed his regret wasn't just an act.

"I really, really tried to make it as painless as possible." He flashed me a weak smile. "But technology has its limits."

My confusion must have showed through the paralysis.

"Electroplating," he explained.

Well, *that* was certainly a new one!

"You'll become a statue. Both beautiful and precious. I managed to...er...liberate a small stash of gold plating. It's not a lot but it's enough, I think, to do you justice. Enough to coat you completely, but not so much that the details won't show through. Besides, as long as the coating is thin enough, the process I'm using will keep you malleable for a while."

Malleable? I had no idea what that meant.

"I'll be able to pose you," he explained. "Until the gold sets up and hardens."

He positioned the nozzle so it pointed directly at my chest, and fiddled with the knobs on the box. When everything was arranged to his satisfaction, he pushed a button. A light mist sprayed across my body. On the bright side, the mist was a refreshing respite from the incessant heat.

"We have time," he assured me, "to get to know each other. Maybe a few hours. I realize that you can't talk while the current's flowing so, I suppose, it'll have to be a monologue."

The cooling mist started to sting a little and demanded more of my attention.

"If only we had met under different circumstances, I think I might have been able to love you."

He leaned over, as if he meant to kiss me, and stopped just outside the range of the golden spray. He was close enough so that the warmth of his breath took the edge off the stinging mist where it settled against my cheek. He was perspiring almost as much as I was. His sweat had smudged the dark makeup around his eyes, and made it run. For the first time, I could clearly see their color.

They were green. Dark green.

And the grassy, heathery musk scent rising from his body was hauntingly familiar.

The shock paralyzed me even more effectively than the electric field. I was stunned when all of the recent events fell horribly, tragically into place. Thanatos' familiarity with Greene Genes research. The powerful attraction we'd felt for each other. My reluctance to beat him to a pulp when I'd had the chance. Suddenly, all of it made sense.

I couldn't help myself; I started to cry.

Thanatos immediately sensed there was something wrong. That is, he sensed there was something wrong *other* than the fact that he was halfway to Simonizing me to death. My tears puzzled him and, now, it was his turn to look deeply into my eyes. I think he understood that there was something important I was trying to tell him, and he was curious about it.

The instant our gazes locked, he froze. He *knew.*

For whatever little of my life I had left, I could not fathom how either one of us was going to extricate ourselves from this terrible situation.

"Alec?" he whispered. Then as the initial surprise faded, he breathed, "Oh, my God!"

Panicked, he jabbed at the buttons on the machine but he

was still reeling with the shock of his discovery. It made him clumsy. I truly believe he intended to turn off the compressor. The spray from the nozzle actually trickled and almost died, but an instant later it started up again, even stronger than before. Even if I'd been able to speak, even if I could have told him he'd accidentally hit the wrong switch, or twisted a knob the wrong way, I was weeping too heavily for him to possibly understand me.

The pain was not physical, but it was no less palpable. I would have gladly perished in excruciating agony if I could only have spared myself what I'd just learned. No matter what happened in the next few minutes, I could never un-know it. All at once, dying as soon as possible seemed a welcome choice.

"Alec," he whispered again, "Oh, Alec! You don't understand."

I didn't, of course. Not yet. Not then. My mind was still struggling with the revelation that the maniac who had held Centerport hostage, who had blown up half a dozen people, who had kidnaped Bradley Harmon and who had, very probably, murdered a man who had been like a father to him, in fact, the same madman who was on the verge of turning me into a garden ornament...was my beloved husband, Peter.

What I did next was perhaps the most difficult thing I'd ever done in my life, not only because I was already grieving, but also because my mouth still wouldn't work. Nevertheless, after tremendous effort, I succeeded in forming a single, garbled word.

"Why?"

Thanatos...*Peter* didn't need to hear me to understand the question. His features twisted with the agony of his emotions and he, too, burst into tears. He formed his hands into fists, crammed his knuckles into his mouth to keep from screaming, and bit down on them hard enough to draw blood. As horrible as it was for me to recognize Thanatos, Peter's turmoil upon realizing that I was the Whirlwind was infinitely worse.

"For you, Alec," he breathed. The words were so incongruous, I thought I'd misheard. "I did it for *you*. For *us*."

If only he'd had the presence of mind to realize the compressor was still going. If only he'd tried to turn off the electrical field again. If only he'd done any one of half a dozen other possible things, maybe everything could have worked out differently. I like to think that's true. But both of us were so wrapped up in our discoveries that neither one stopped to consider that I was still trapped and unable to move.

"I love you, Alec. You know that. You *have* to know that!"

Neck muscles straining, I managed to incline my head a fraction of an inch. Encouraged, he went on.

"Oh, my sweet baby, when I found you, when I first saw you, do you know what I thought?"

I waited, figuring he'd tell me even if I couldn't shake my head.

"I thought, there is the most amazing and beautiful man I have ever seen. After that first night, I knew it wasn't just on the surface. It goes all the way through. To here."

He made as if to place his palm on the center of my chest but he snatched his hand away. I understood my husband well enough to know that it had nothing to do with the current. He was afraid to touch me, afraid he'd further defile our relationship. He was embarrassed and ashamed of himself.

"The very next morning, I knew I *had* to spend the rest of my life with you. That's the God's honest truth. I knew it *that* soon."

His head bobbed up and down rapidly as if, by nodding so strenuously, he would make what he said even more true. With a frisson of unease, I saw that his eyes held more than a hint of hysteria in them.

"But you were a hooker, Alec. A *whore*!"

He spat the word. My heart felt like it was being crushed like an old tin can.

There are certain moments in everyone's life that we remember as if they were orchestrated by Disney. We imagine that there's music swelling and that little cartoon bunnies and butterflies are cavorting just outside the frame. The day I met Peter, I'd felt like that.

"I thought to myself, how can I possibly marry *him*?"

The bunnies fell dead; the butterflies fell to the ground with shriveled wings; the strings on the violins warped and snapped.

"But I still loved you! So, I did it anyway. But then, Alec… then…"

He was still wearing that awful skull mask so I couldn't see the nuances of his expression, but something struck me as terribly, terribly wrong. There was an unsettling tightness in his voice, and a glint of irrational panic in his eye. I was suddenly far more afraid for him than I was for myself. If I could have spoken, I would have told him that everything would be all right.

It would have been a lie, but I would have said it anyway.

"Then Ritchie passed that ridiculous law. Just when I thought we could have a normal life, that we could put your ugly past behind us, you opened the agency. You went from whore to pimp, Alec. How was I supposed to deal with that? You're my *husband*, for Christ's sake!"

Peter clenched his fists and threw back his head. Every muscle in his neck was corded with tension when he gave vent to a terrifying shriek of abject misery.

"You didn't *have* to work, Alec! You had Mary's. We could have re-opened it if you wanted, or if you felt you *needed* something to keep you busy. We would have been happier, so much happier, if you'd just stayed home and given up that filthy rotten business. Even if you just hung around the house all day. I would have found a way to make sure that the only thing you had to do was love me."

My head was spinning and I had cramps in my stomach. Neither had anything to do with the fact that I was being encased in precious metal. I continued to sob. Even when the tiny particles of gold clogged my tear ducts, I wept on the inside.

"I did it for the money, Alec. That was the only reason. I planned on telling you that I'd inherited it from some relative I never knew I had. You never would have found out how much it really was. It would have been enough… *Enough!*"

He shouted that last.

"Enough for you to quit the agency. Enough for us to move away. Some place with a beach. Anywhere! Just as long as it was far enough so that neither of us would ever have to look at a street corner where you once *prostituted* yourself and feel ashamed by it. Far enough so that we wouldn't be tarnished by those memories."

Tarnished?

How could I have been so oblivious, so stupid? I'd thought our marriage was perfect. Yet, since the very day we met, Peter had been unable to get past my being a rent boy. Why did he never say anything? If I'd only known, I would have done anything he wanted. I'd have given up the agency in a heartbeat. He'd have only had to ask.

But he hadn't.

Even though my heart was breaking, I couldn't keep a righteous anger from bubbling up. All those years ago, I took to the streets because I hadn't had a choice. I wasn't much more than a kid when my parents threw me out. Travis tried to help me out, but I was still raw from my family. I thought the only person you could rely on was yourself.

And dammit, I had!

Not only did I survive, I thrived. Now, I had a respectable business to show for it! How dare Peter look at me like I was filth, like everything I'd worked for was something tawdry and dirty? If I'd been able to speak, God knows what I would have said to him. Awful things probably, things that I would have regretted.

Fortunately, the field kept me mute. I could only whimper and, in a few seconds, my rage faded and I was left feeling empty and numb.

"We can't…*I* can't go on like this Alec. I could have *killed* you, baby! I'd cut my own arms and legs off before I'd let anything hurt you!"

He bent toward me as if for a kiss, but the electric field stopped him. He drew back and seemed confused, as if he didn't know what he should do next. His eyelids fluttered beneath the mask, as if he was blinking in confusion. Then he became quite still and stood for a long time, doing nothing more than looking down at my helpless body. It was then that it truly dawned on him what he'd almost done, what he *had* done.

He clenched both fists and his body stiffened. His shriek

was even louder and more tortured than before. Looking back, I desperately want to believe that it was the sound of Peter's mind refusing to cope, that in that moment something inside him broke. I pray that the part of him that I loved simply...went away, and that he no longer knew what he was doing.

But I'll never be sure.

He moved outside my field of vision. I had no idea what he intended to do, but I knew that one of us would regret it. A few moments later, I heard his voice coming from high above me. With a Herculean effort I managed to move my head just enough to catch a glimpse of him from the corner of my eye. He had finally cast that horrid mask aside and stood on a catwalk some twenty or thirty feet above the foundry floor. The light from the vat of molten liquid below him washed over his body in its black costume. He looked like the glistening statue of a young god carved from flawless onyx.

"I love you, Alec!" he cried. "I want you to always remember that!"

I tried to close my eyes. I didn't want to see what came next. At the same time, I wanted to keep looking at Peter for as long as possible. I think I knew it would be my last chance.

His dive was as perfect as that of any Olympic champion. Peter's body arched into the air and unfolded beautifully, a moving work of art. He soared below my line of sight and I knew he was gone. There was not even a splash to mark his passing, only the furnace which coincidentally belched a little before subsiding. Fortunately, he didn't scream.

I don't think I could have handled it if he had.

I lay there for hours, imagining I could feel the molecules of gold adhering to my skin. The pain was minor at first, but soon became unbearable, even through the suit. A fusillade of red-hot microscopic pellets seemed to sand-blast my skin, flaying me alive. Even worse was the pain of Peter's last words, gnawing at my soul.

Whore, he'd called me, and *pimp*.

I didn't want to die; I wanted to be already dead. If I could have gotten free, I honestly can't say that I would not have hurled myself into the same vat as Peter had. Maybe, if I forced myself to stay beneath the molten metal for long enough, I could accomplish what the Caterpillar and the Marauder and all the others had failed to do. Maybe the atoms that had once made up Alec Archer would be broken down and dissipated in the fiery liquid. Maybe they would mingle with the atoms that had once been part of Peter Camry. Eventually, when the sludge cooled, maybe Peter and I would be inextricably linked for all time.

Neither Man nor God would be able to separate us. There were less desirable ways I could have chosen to spend eternity.

A long time later, the gold ran out. The machine continued to try and pump nothingness and, with no one to turn it off, the compressor eventually overheated. I smelled the oily smoke before I saw it, but I found it impossible to care. When it blew up, I only half noticed. It wasn't until the flames reached me that I paid any attention at all. Even then, it was only to urge them to burn hotter in the hope that, by some miracle, they would sear away the deeper pain.

The foundry had been built to withstand high temperatures, but its architects had never anticipated an inferno like this. Glass flowed from the windows like water and anything that wasn't metal was reduced to ash. When the structural supports warped and collapsed, the roof caved in and provided more fuel to the blaze. Only some of the vats, the ones built to contain molten metal, survived.

And me, of course. Pity.

I have a dim recollection of hearing sirens, barely discernable over the fire's roar. I'm told it was one of the worst conflagrations Centerport had ever seen. It raged through the night and well into the next morning before it was extinguished. Close to a dozen firefighters were injured. When a police officer spotted Thanatos' scooter parked near the building, Gretchen called Travis. The two of them spent several harried days, waiting for the wreckage to cool down enough so they could search for my body.

Poetically, it was Travis who found me. In his protective clothing, he looked like a huge silver version of the Pillsbury Dough Boy. He was crying behind the plastic mask when he lifted me in his burly arms. I remember wondering if he was so upset because I'd damaged the Whirlwind's suit again. At some point, the heat had been intense enough to defeat even Travis' ingenuity. The fabric had literally boiled away from my skin. I was stark naked when he carried me from the wreckage. It took some doing on Gretchen's part to make sure that photos of the Whirlwind's junk weren't displayed on the front page of the *Courier*.

For days, I drifted in and out of consciousness. Though my body was severely damaged, I overheard Travis tell Gretchen that the worst injuries were emotional. Physically, I appeared to heal in a remarkably short period of time, even for me. Nevertheless, there was some residual trauma that wasn't as obvious as burn scars would have been. For months afterward, I would be doing something mundane like making a cup of coffee and my hands would start to shake. The cup would smash and I'd find myself on my hands and knees, weeping uncontrollably while I struggled to clean up the mess. Travis claimed there was nothing organically wrong with me, but I knew better.

What could be more organic than a ravaged soul?

CHAPTER TWENTY

B itter is as bitter does, as I always say. Actually, I don't always say that. In fact, I've never said it before. But I've been thinking it a lot lately.

Cleaning up after Thanatos went without a hitch. Bradley Harmon had little difficulty synthesizing a cure for the cops who'd been infected at Lacey's Farm. Completely removing the Three-Two-Three variant from the virus was a different matter altogether. When Doctor Harmon's "breakthrough" turned out to be a bust, he decided the Feed the World Project, no matter how well-intentioned, was too dangerous to pursue. Greene Genes shelved it indefinitely.

Everyone assumed that Peter had been killed by Thanatos. In a way, that was true. Ironically, when Herman Starcke took the reins of the company, it turned out that he might not have hated Peter as much as we'd thought. Gretchen reported that Herman got very teary while he was delivering the funeral elegy, and he certainly wasn't the type to fake emotion.

I wouldn't know. I couldn't watch while they buried an empty box in front of a stone with my husband's name chiseled into it. I still haven't been to the cemetery. Every week, Travis dutifully places a bunch of roses atop the grave and signs my name to the card.

It's not because I hate Peter; that will never be true. But the wounds are still too fresh. The first time I resolved to visit the cemetery, I couldn't even make it past the front door.

While the ghost of Peter's presence still permeates Ale Mary's, it doesn't bother me. Together, we banished all of the bad memories the place held from my childhood and made it into our haven. Besides, though there was a lot of deception, nothing bad between us ever happened within these walls.

Business at the Archer Agency is booming. In fact, after Peter vanished, it picked up. Many of my old friends seemed to think that throwing clients my way to keep me busy might help ease the loss. Even Irving Tressman walked on eggshells for a couple of months. They're all wrong if they think I'm wallowing. I just need some more time to process, as they say, before I feel myself again.

As for the Whirlwind, he seems to be doing okay. The guy's a hero after all. And heroes don't cry, do they?

Not even when they want to.

Look for the next Alex Archer adventure:

A STUDY IN SPANDEX

Available Spring 2021

ABOUT THE AUTHOR

Hal Bodner is the author of the best-selling gay vampire novel *Bite Club* and the lupine sequel *The Trouble With Hairy*. He tells people that he was born in East Philadelphia because no one knows where Cherry Hill, New Jersey is. The obstetrician who delivered him was C. Everett Koop, the future U.S. Surgeon General who put warnings on cigarette packs. Thus, from birth, Hal was destined to become a heavy smoker.

He moved to West Hollywood in the 1980s and has rarely left the city limits since. He cannot even find his way around Beverly Hills—which is the next town over.

Hal has been an entertainment lawyer, a scheduler for a 976 sex telephone line, a theater reviewer, and the personal assistant to a television star. For a while, he owned Heavy Petting, a pet boutique where all the movie stars shopped for their Pomeranians. Until recently, he owned an exotic bird shop.

He has never been a waiter.

He lives with assorted dogs and birds, the most notable of which is an eighty-year-old, irritable, flesh-eating military macaw named after his icon—Tallulah. He often quips he is a slave to fur and feathers and regrets only that he isn't referring to mink and marabou. He does not have cats because he tends to sneeze on them.

Having reached middle age, he remembers Nixon.

He was widowed in his early forties and can sometimes be found sunbathing at his late partner's grave while trying to avoid cemetery caretakers screaming at him to put his shirt back on.

Hal has also written a few erotic paranormal romances—which he refers to as "supernatural smut"—most notably *In Flesh and Stone* and *For Love of the Dead*. While his salacious imagination is unbounded, he much prefers his comedic roots and he is currently pecking away at a series of bitterly humorous gay superhero novels.

He has married again—this time legally—to a wonderful man who is young enough not to know that Liza Minnelli is Judy Garland's daughter. As a result, Hal has recently discovered that the use of hair dye is rarely an adequate substitute for Viagra.

Hal's website is www.wehovampire.com and he encourages fans to send him email at Hal@wehovampire.com. It may take him a month or so, but he generally responds to almost everyone who writes to him with the sole exception of prisoners who request free copies of his books accompanied by naked pictures.

OTHER BOOKS BY HAL BODNER

A Study in Spandex
Bite Club
Fabulous in Tights
For Love of the Dead
In Flesh and Stone
The Trouble with Hairy

Curious about other Crossroad Press books?
Stop by our site:
http://store.crossroadpress.com
We offer quality writing
in digital, audio, and print formats.

CPSIA information can be obtained
at www.ICGtesting.com
Printed in the USA
FSHW022000120122
87623FS